Reasons for Hope:

Speculative stories and poems

The Writing Journey

06 August 2017

Other projects of the Writing Journey

Infinite Monkeys (2009), edited by Katherine Lato

The Letter (2012), edited by Claire Somersville

Drops of Midnight (2012), edited by Steven White

The Day Before the End of the World (2012), edited by Roger Lubeck

Stories from Other Worlds (2014), edited by Roger Lubeck and Ana Koulouris

Voices from the Dark (2015), edited by Roger C. Lubeck, Phoenix Autumn, Ana Koulouris, Sara Marschand, and Kevin C. Swier.

Human: An Exploration of What It Means (2016), Edited by Tim Yao, Melinda Borucki and Mary O'Brien Glatz

Near Myths (2017), Edited by Awnna Marie Evans, Eleanor Roth, Todd Hogan and Tim Yao

See *writingjourney.org/books/* for a complete, up-to-date list.

Reasons for Hope

Edited by Tim Yao, Sara Vallejo and Mary O'Brien Glatz

Copy editing by Mary O'Brien-Glatz and Sara Vallejo

This Anthology is a project of the Writing Journey (writingjourney.org)

ISBN: 9781791825010

Cover Design by Tim Yao

Contents

Afterword

Acknowledgements

The Editors of this anthology would like to thank the hard work by Sara Vallejo and Mary O'Brien-Glatz to copy edit the stories.

Many thanks as well to Patti Naisbitt, Program Coordinator of the Woodridge Public Library, and to Amy Franco, Adult Programming Librarian of the Glen Ellyn Public Library, for their generous support as sponsors of the Writing Journey.

Introduction

The proverbial wellspring of hope can serve as an antidote to personal and collective despair. What is hope? Where does it come from? How does it manifest?

Do the origins of hope change over time and context?

Albert Camus reminds us that in particularly dark and uncertain times we are called to stretch our minds to reach for something better, bigger, nobler, grander. When we witness suffering on personal, societal, environmental, and cultural landscapes, are we capable of expanding our imaginations, hearts and resources to create anew?

In the midst of despair, perhaps a profound shift can stimulate hope and thus action. Is uncertainty itself a necessary and sufficient condition for hope to arise, for it provides an otherwise unavailable spaciousness into which new possibilities spring forth? The space of new frontiers.

The authors in this anthology compassionately offer answers to these questions in creative short stories and poems. Speculative fiction spans the range of science fiction, fantasy, tales of superheroes and heroines, magical realism, horror, utopian and dystopian worlds, and the supernatural. These stories and poems traverse the broad arc of the speculative fiction imagination to suggest diverse possibilities for hope. They serve up entertaining and perhaps viable alternatives to real personal and communal problems of our world today. Step into this space and experience a myriad of reasons to hope in our human capacity to change, explore, connect, correct, love, heal, and create anew.

Other writers have addressed this elusive topic of hope. Rebecca Solnit, in *Hope in the Dark*, suggests that in both private, personal depression and in the collective conscience, the acute pain of the present brings paralysis. She suggests that,

> *"Hope is an embrace of the unknown and the unknowable, an
> alternative to the certainty of both optimists and pessimists. Op-*

timists think it will all be fine without our involvement; pessimists take the opposite position; both excuse themselves from acting. It's the belief that what we do matters even though how and when it may matter, who and what it may impact, are not things we can know beforehand."

The colorful stories in this collection are tales of actions that catalyze change for the better, that visualize in words for us the results of deeds springing forth from chasms of uncertainty into spaces of hope. Each story is distinct in its depiction of potential antidotes to despair and destruction. Their common root runs deep in the human character, in its individual ingenuity and its collective drive toward solutions for what ails us now and what could destroy us in the future. In these stories and poems, individual and communal actions feed the wellspring of hope, enact the changes that allow us to be unstuck, to move forward into the possibility of the unknown, to leave the mire of despair behind, to save the day.

The characters that spring forth from these pages are intelligent, brave, heroic, compassionate, loving, kind, determined, creative, and loyal, despite their dire circumstances. Their actions are sometimes small and tender, as in taking the hand of a little girl who is grieving, sometimes grand, bold, epic, as in saving the planet despite extreme personal risk and bodily harm, sometimes brilliant, industrious, dedicated, as in finding a solution to rising seas left unchecked by global warming, sometimes scientific or technological as in building brave new worlds. All are valorous, valiant, ennobling, uplifting, and spring into action as they leap into the unknown with the courage of the human heart.

Victor Frankl suggests that idealism is the best kind of realism in our search for, and the only choice in achieving, meaning in life, particularly in times when meaning seems lost. If hope is the result of consciously choosing intelligent idealism in the midst of tumultuous defeatism, the writers in this collection deliver just that - intelligent idealism. They ask us to consider ideas that some may deem far fetched, outrageous, ridiculous.

The stories in this anthology give us a glimpse of new possibilities, new creations, and new constructions that spring from the imaginations of a talented group of budding writers, the members of The Writing Journey.

Hope is an embrace of the unknown and the unknowable. We don't know what will happen, but the space of uncertainty gives hope room to act. When uncertain, hope is a belief that we might impact the outcomes of an unknown future. Some might call it faith to leap into the unknown. Others might call it grit. All acknowledge its possibility.

We invite you to savor these stories and poems exploring *Reasons to Hope* - hope in the ugly, the deformed, the unwanted, the small, the magical, the impossible, the brave, the improbable, the inventive, the scientific, the technological. Anything is possible with time travel to correct the past and shape the future, virtual puppies to soften human cruelty, magic therapy boxes to erase despair, artificial islands to save a homeland, intergalactic travel to bring world peace, accessing akashic fourth dimensions to change the present, and of course deepening our relationship with ourselves, others and our animal friends.

These stories offer fictional mentats for what ails us now in this time, as well as in our past and future times. Join us. Step into the unknown with us. Savor the Possibilities and Hope for the best. It was an honor and a pleasure to edit this fine collection of Speculative Fiction Stories and Poems, *Reasons to Hope*, by The Writing Journey.

by Mary O'Brien-Glatz

13th Persian poem of unknown origin

Some nights stay up 'til dawn
as the moon sometimes does for the sun.
Be a full bucket pulled up in the dark
the way of a well when lifted out into the light.
Something opens our wings,
Something makes boredom and hurt disappear.
Someone fills the cup in front of us,
and we taste only sacredness.

Shotai's Song

Diana Jean

My serial number is MH24-30434-384795-38. My manufacturing date is Earth 3012-05-04. I was produced at Watanabe Labs Inc in Osaka, Japan under the product name Shotai Maintenance v. 4.5. I was installed onto *The Sacagawea*, an American military cargo vessel, on Earth 10-07-3012, to perform basic sanitation and maintenance for the crew quarters. I was updated with the artificial intelligence program Cambre A.I. v. 15.3 so that I could perform my duties without human assistance or supervision.

The Sacagawea left the American Lunar Spaceport on Earth 3012-08-10.

My display read: *At ship time 0800, I was released from my charging platform to perform my routine cleanings functions. I proceeded to the communal observation deck, mess hall, kitchens, and Docking Bay 7. At 1800, I proceeded to officer quarters, Deck 5, to begin my duties of-*

"Wait," Lieutenant Northway interrupted, waving a hand. Seated on her desk chair, she leaned close so she could read the text display on my screen. "Why do you clean the rooms here so late?"

I have uploaded the current schedule for all officers on board. This is your designated meal hour.

Lieutenant Northway sighed, briefly lowering her head between her knees. "Guess your schedule didn't say that I get space sick..." She looked up and wrinkled her nose in frustration. Part of my A.I. program was reading human expression, to ease communication.

I waited four tics before I concluded that Lieutenant Northway was not going to continue her statement. *It is advisable that you visit the sick bay for illnesses.*

"It's only a passing thing. Give me a day and I'll be fine."

Would you like to schedule a time for me to return?

She smiled. "Stay, please. I'm just catching up on some reading."

I gave a soft beep of acknowledgment, then turned to assess the room. I would have to create a special routine for Lieutenant Northway's room, since I would not be able to clean the space around her desk. I made the appropriate adjustments and began to move away.

"Wait."

I stopped and turned.

"Do you... talk at all?"

I do not have a functional A.I. voice. My sounds are restricted to the standards of Shotai Maintenance v. 4.5. They are as follows; an acknowledgment. I made the beep. *An alert.* I produced harsh chirp. *An emergency call.* My siren blared.

Lieutenant Northway quickly waved her hands. "That's enough. Thank you!"

You are most welcome, Lieutenant Northway.

She smiled, rubbing her forehead. "Just Marissa. Your display is small enough without my full name and title crowding it."

You are most welcome, Marissa.

She gave a soft laugh. "Okay, what can I call you? So I don't have to shout 'robot!' and get thirty machines looking at me."

I am Shotai Maintenance v. 4.5.

She pressed a finger to her lips, humming softly. "How about Shotai? Will you answer to that?"

No one had ever attempted to name me before. It took a moment to process the request. *I will answer to Shotai.*

Marissa grinned, leaning back in her chair. "Good. Well, you may continue with your work, Shotai."

I turned and continued my tasks, making adjustments in my schedule for the delay so that I would be back in my charging port before 2100.

"Play some music, Shotai?" Marissa asked as I deposited her soiled laundry into the chute exactly 24.34 hours since our last communication.

Another request that I had never been given before. Most humans on the ship played music through their personal entertainment devices. I had already cataloged that Marissa had such a device on her desk.

I had the ability to play music. I could access the ship's main computers and download any non-confidential programs. This included crew entertainment and the expansive catalog of musical programs. It took ten tics before I answered with a soft beep and began to play the program that had been accessed most frequently: Wind Sand by Atotoztli Kovacevic. A fast, loud instrumental piece from the 4th Colony on Io.

The song only played for 32 tics before Marissa spoke. "No, not that. Maybe something more comforting? Classical?"

I did not know how to catalog songs by 'comforting,' but the database did have Classical. I chose a program at random: Sonata in A major, movement I by Wolfgang Amadeus Mozart.

Marissa bobbed her head with the music, humming to the pitch of some of the notes. There were no human vocals in the song. I paused in my cleaning, trying to compute how Marissa chose the notes to sing.

Marissa noticed my lapse in work. "Something wrong?"

I rolled forward so she could easily read my screen. *What are you singing?*

Apparently my question was new to her, because Marissa took twelve tics to answer. "Well, I'm singing to the melody. Or trying to, anyway." She leaned forward. "Don't tell anyone about my lousy singing, okay?" She winked.

My privacy setting forbids me from disclosing personal information on any officer or crew aboard.

She smiled. "Good. Since I know you're safe, play me something that I can really sing along with."

I selected again from the Classical database, since Marissa did not specify that I look elsewhere. I organized the selection by instrumentation and chose one at random that included human vocals. I chose *Dido's Lament Aria* from Henry Purcell's *Dido and Aeneas*.

A woman's voice emitted from my speakers. She was soft, voice quivering.

When I am laid, am laid in earth, May my wrongs create
No trouble, no trouble in thy breast;
Remember me, remember me, but ah! forget my fate.

The instruments swelled and fell with her singing, but they were simple against the tone of her powerful voice. They supported her as she rose in volume, then suddenly died away. I could access the context for the piece, the history of the composer, history of the subject. I could find research on the meaning of the lyrics, or commentaries of the entire opera.

Yet, as the voice grew to a high, trembling pitch, before fading away, the instruments following into the silence, I did not perform these actions. Instead, I remained motionless. My A.I. program made a soft whirring noise as I processed the music. I almost repeated the piece, though Marissa did not give me the order. I almost had the *need* to repeat it. A need not dissimilar to my needs to perform my assigned tasks or my need to return to my charging port at the end of the night. It was strange to see such an action item in my coding that was not programmed there. It had been created by my A.I. By *me*, in response to the music.

Marissa was staring at me. "Are you okay, Shotai?"

I hadn't moved since the song had started, and it had been twenty-five tics since it ended. *I am functioning adequately, Marissa.*

She still looked worried. "Did you... like the piece?"

I had never liked or disliked anything. Everything was categorized by it meeting my programmed requirements or not. Music technically did not meet my requirements. However, that was not the question Marissa had asked.

I will process it. I answered, and then proceeded to play the piece again. I continued with my work, calculating again with the delay. However, I made sure to keep the music repeating, even as I left Marissa's quarters to my next task.

It is a sad piece, I reported 23.78 hours later.

It was about human lamentations and death. It was played in a minor key, the notes always cascading down into barely resolved chords. It was, by many musical definitions of that time period and location, a sad piece.

Marissa laughed. She was eating now, though she chose to take her meals in her room. I had asked her once again if she wished I would arrive at another time. She declined my offer. "Well, of course it is a sad piece! But do you like it?"

I hesitated five tics. *The female singer is lamenting, but her voice has such strength. It is not unsatisfying.*

"That means you like it." Marissa speared her salad with her fork. "Have you been listening to anything else?"

Yes, I have analyzed the entire classic opera genre available in the ship's database.

Her eyes widened. "All in one day?"

If not played aloud, I am able to skim through the songs at an accelerated pace.

She waved her fork. "Well, that's not right. You have to experience the song, not just blow through it! Okay, play me your favorite."

I had no concept of a 'favorite,' but I played the song that I had repeated the most. It was *Deh Vieni, Non Tardar*, Susanna's Aria from Wolfgang Amadeus Mozart's *Le Nozze di Figaro*.

The orchestra seemed to bounce in. The strings light on their notes. I had done more research into the various components that made up classic opera. The clear soprano sang from my speakers. Marissa put down her fork and folded her hands.

"That is very beautiful. *The Marriage of Figaro*, right?" She hummed slightly. Then she opened her mouth to softly sing the words.

Qui mormora il ruscel, qui scherza l'aura

Che col dolce susurro il cor ristaura

There was something right about Marissa singing. It made the pre-recorded voice more alive. It made it feel as if the performance was happening in the quarters, instead of emitted from my speakers.

Marissa suddenly stood. "Come with me."

I had never left my post before my assigned task was complete, but Marissa had given me a direct order. I logged the delay and followed her. Marissa walked purposefully down the hall, her boots clicking in the metal floors. She stopped and entered a nearby door, an observation room.

I followed on her heels. It was a simple room with a large table, some chairs, a few couches, and a few low tables. I checked it every night to make sure it was clean.

Marissa went to stand by one of the large windows. Space blazed past in a swirl of stars, galaxies, planets, and asteroids as the ship traveled through a slip stream faster than the speed of light. I knew it was all an optical illusion, the walls of the stream casting reflections of celestial bodies that could be 200 light years away.

Marissa touched the window and inhaled deeply. When she opened her mouth, she sang.

Sasi sasi ae taro taro amu

Her voice wavered and her breaths were louder than the voices I had listened to previously. She also sang in a language I did not recognized, despite having nearly 4,000 languages and dialects programmed.

Marissa turned, her voice a little stronger.

Sasi sasi ae na ga koro mi koro

I understood why she had brought me here. In the cramped walls of her quarters, my speakers sounded tinny and flat. Here, in the more open space of the observation room, the acoustics were stronger, carrying her voice, even as she wavered.

She finished, voice trailing and smiled at me. "You should play your music wherever you are. See if you can find places like this, places that really do it justice."

What was that piece you just sang?

She had to take a few steps closer to read my display. "A lullaby called *Rorogwela*. It's from the Solomon Islands, on Earth. It is not a language that is spoken anymore. At the time the song was recorded, very few people spoke it. It's... actually what made me decide to become a linguist. I heard so many of these dead languages and I wanted to learn all that I could. Even if I became the only one who still understood."

What do the words mean?

"It is about a crying child and about comfort during a time of great hardship." She leaned over and touched the top of my display. "You should try all sorts of songs, Shotai. From different people, different cultures, different worlds. Sing it all around the ship." She winked. "And tell me where the best acoustics are, okay?"

The more I listened to music, the more I learned. My hard drive constantly ran hot, storing and analyzing the information I received. Following Marissa's guidance, I listened to music from all over Earth and its colonies. I listened to the chants from Mars' first colony, dry and as grating as the red desert. I listened to folk music from Bangladesh, songs of freedom and oppression by a man named Lalon. I listened to music from the Navajo nation in America, drumbeats like human hearts and chanting voices strong in celebration. I listened to a man recite Ya Sin from the Qu'ran, his voice deep, guttural, and unwavering as he spoke his faith. I listened to jiuta music from Japan, a piercing, warbling voice accompanied only by a koto, shamisen, and flute. Singing a tune so old that no one knows who wrote it, only that it is for dancing.

I played out my music from my small speakers as I worked. Other members of the crew began to notice me and my music. They called out to me in the halls, made requests, offered their opinion on the piece I was currently playing.

I began to choose songs that displayed the most of human passions. Like Dido's Lament with great sadness. Arias singing of true love. Voices singing in celebration, in justice. Those were the words that fell into my repeat list. The words that I understood in every language. Or, like Rorogwela, which I did not need to translate to understand.

I could now choose what a comforting song would be. Or an exciting one, a stirring one. A song to make humans slow their steps and sway their heads.

I found that the mess hall would make my music reverberate, but often it was too full of people for proper projection. The cargo bays were larger, their high ceilings echoing and jumbling the notes around the metal walls. I tried every observation room, conference room, the recreation room, crew quarters, offices, and even sick bay. The words flowing from me and through the ship.

Yume no urakata echigo no shishi wa
Tare dhorte parle mono bedi
Che gelida manina,
'Tis the gift to be simple,

There was something that I required from these songs. Something that I hadn't computed yet. Something that made me play them over and over again. As if I was searching for the one piece of music that would make me sing as pure and unfiltered as Marissa in the observation room. As soft as when she hummed at her desk. As bold as when she walked with me through the halls, singing to an aria from Italy or a folk song from Japan or a chant from Mars.

Every day I would come to her room and we would discuss the pieces

I had been listening to. Often it was something new that I had dredged up from the database. Sometimes it was an old piece that I could not leave alone in my memory drive. My work efficiency plummeted and I was brought to IT to be reevaluated. When Officer Nakamura recognized me as the robot who 'played the tunes,' I was released without change. Other Shotai Maintenance v. 4.5 were sent out to cover more of my areas.

Sometimes, often after recharging, when it would be silent in the maintenance bay, I tried to sing. My limited vocalizations did not produce much variety or tone, nor did I have control over volume. I could project innumerable voices from across the centuries, but I had no voice of my own.

The Sacagawea arrived at Leonidas Beta, a small brown planet orbiting the blue star Maia in the Pleiades system. Much of the cargo would be deposited at several colonies located on the planet, and at least half of the crew would remain once the *Sacagawea* had left.

Marissa was to stay on the planet as Chief Linguist and liaison between the new colonies. She would serve there for three years and then be shipped back to Earth on the next military supply ship. I would remain on the *Sacagawea* until I malfunctioned or became otherwise useless. I did not know where the *Sacagawea* would go once it left Leonidas Beta.

Marissa took me from the ship soon after it landed. I had not been given an assignment for the day as unloading people and cargo would cause too much traffic for me to work adequately.

Marissa took me into a transport pod with her as we made our descent to the planet. I could not see out the port windows, so Marissa described the planet to me. "It does not have the oceans or large lakes of Earth, but it does have many rivers, constantly flowing in and around each other, cutting deep rocky canyons. Most people live in the valley of the canyons, where the heat from the star is not so intense. I visited here once before, years ago. I always wondered what it would be like to stay."

We landed and I soon discovered that the uneven ground was difficult for my delicate wheels. Marissa leaned down, putting a hand behind my display screen and helped me along.

"It is not too far." She grinned.

I felt the grit in my wheels, every bump that battered into my metal exterior.

The docking port for the pods and other small ships was loud and busy with people. Marissa quickly guided me away, past some fences, a marked gate, down a winding path. I concentrated on not upsetting my internal balance, navigating a narrow dirt path lined with rocks, shrubs, and a rather steep cliff. The voices of humans and machines faded. They were replaced by animal noises, clicks, growls, and calls that were not in my memory storage.

Marissa hummed as we walked and, as we descended, her voice began to reverberate. It echoed, but not so uncontrolled like in the cargo bay. We went into a narrow canyon. When we reached the bottom, Marissa led me forward, passing by a small creek that was little more than a trickle. The ground was sandy and damp, the walls of the canyon stretched above, almost curving over. Marissa continued to hum and she grew a little louder, then stopped.

"Here. This is a good spot."

Then she sang.

How pleasant thy banks and green valleys below,
Where, wild in the woodlands, the primroses blow

Her voice echoed around. It filled the dark air around us, climbed up the walls. and settled in soft echoes. The stream was a whisper to her voice. The animals quieted by the new sound in their space.

Sweet Afton by Robert Burns. I displayed. *That is not a song. It is a poem.*

Marissa turned to read. "Yes, but often songs come from poetry. Sometimes they have a tune that everyone knows. Sometimes you just make it up as you go. Just because you love the words and speaking is just not enough."

Not enough. Perhaps that is what I was searching for. Something that was enough to fill me. Something like the singing that I couldn't perform.

Marissa, if I displayed words, would you sing them?

She knelt beside me. "Of course, Shotai. Are you telling me that you wrote something?"

She was asking if I created something, something that only I could make, something that would not exist without me. Maybe I couldn't sing, but not all humans sang either. Sometimes they had to find others to give them music.

I displayed.

If I had a voice it would be strong,
strong enough to break free of space
echo around moons and planets and stars.
My voice, even from across a galaxy,
would be able to find
wherever you sing for me.

Marissa made it soft and slow, but with the strength of that soprano who sang *Dido's Lament*, the first song that challenged my program. Marissa opened her mouth wide and sang for the whole canyon, so strong that if the people unloading the ship had stopped and listened, they would be able to hear it. Her voice skimmed over the creek and bubbled in tune with her melody. Her voice echoed against rock and bounced back like she was many voices. Her voice disappeared into the sky.

I recorded her singing. I recorded her every breath of inhalation. When her pitch cracked, pushed too high. When her voice drifted to a whisper so soft that only beside her I could find it.

For many years I would travel across light years of space, long after my warranty expired, long after newer Shotai Maintenance machines were created and installed. I would grind my way back and forth across the ship, my wheels worn. I would play music for anyone who would listen. I would hear hundreds more human voices. I would discover new songs every day and listen to them until every note and word found a place in my programming.

During quiet hours, when the ship's low humming was the only sound for hallway after empty hallway, I would find a secluded observation deck. There I would play Marissa's voice, singing loud and clear even with so much space and time between us. Perhaps I never needed to learn to sing.

I had found my song.

Island

Tim Yao

Breathe the warm air—taste the ocean in it.
Open your eyes, see the blue green of the waters around you.
This is the island of my people, an island slowly vanishing as
      the sea level rises.

Many on my island gave up, fled to safety.
They abandoned their way of life to fill crowded refugee camps.

The talkers who promised help were nowhere to be found.

Only memories sustained me for years.
My mother and sisters, poor beyond words, stayed behind.
I traveled on, driven by my test scores and buoyed by my
      mother's faith.

Now, the sea is everywhere.

Driven by my family's plight and my people's need,
I studied microbiology and genetic engineering.
We created life: a robust, simplified form of coral
that fed upon vast tracts of plastics to grow a floating base
      for new land.

Anchored to the island of my people, it creates hope.

Would it scale? Skeptics abound but engineers found the gaps
    and fixed them.
Some of the wealthy were inspired to finance the solution.
Robots gathered sea trash; ships brought materials.
The land began to take shape around the island's dwindling
    shores.

Earth from our island transforms these floating roseate coral
    sections.
Soon verdant life begins to creep across the land.
The island extends to more than three times its original size,
safely floating atop the waves.

We sell some land to the wealthy to rebuild and bring jobs.

Today, our first island gives birth to hope that will save many
    lands.
We recycle to create new homes, new schools.
We can provide hope and land and life to those who feared
    the worst.

Now, on a new beach, I hug my mother for the first time in
    years.
She looks so small and frail as her tears wet my cheeks.
My sisters, all grown up, crowd around us, smile and hug me.

We are together again.

Claire

Todd Hogan

On the third day of Dan's recurring exile to the hospital waiting room, he found it occupied. A girl no more than five years old sat in one of the uncomfortable chairs with her head down, poking a handheld tablet. Her honey-blond hair reminded Dan of parks and playgrounds and the shimmer that the summer sun gives to little kids' heads. Across from him, the girl's grandmother waited nervously. Her black-dyed hair lay stiff as straw, caused by long-term oxygenation and hydration in these colonies. Her face was deeply lined and her eyes were hollows. Original colonists had aged poorly due to the scarcity of water for moisturizing and tears. She sat on an unyielding sofa, reluctant to make eye contact. The girl who slouched to Dan's left, swung her legs.

The waiting room felt like it was stuffed with invisible cotton. It slowed movement and muted sounds. Dan hated its mauve walls and the abstract prints on them. He shifted his weight several times. A display rack of pamphlets and brochures offered every kind of assistance and counseling, except the kind that would result in a cure.

After a few silent minutes, the ward nurse poked her head in. The grandmother spoke quietly to the nurse so that the little girl would not overhear. No tears leaked from her tired eyes, though her shoulders sagged. The girl noticed her grandmother's conversation, and put her tablet aside. She slid from her chair, but the grandmother stopped her.

"I'll be right back, dear," she said. She studied Dan until the nurse, who knew him, asked him quietly if he would care for the little girl.

Dan said, "I'll watch her. For a little bit."

The grandmother mouthed a thank you, and with a handkerchief in her hand, hurried out. Her granddaughter sat down again, and twisted her tablet sideways and lengthwise.

Dan and his sister Ava had emigrated with the Third Wave of Martian Settlements twenty years ago. Ava, a classical violinist, played with the Colonial Symphony before it was abandoned for lack of critical mass—musicians, patrons or funds. Dan had attended Ava's performances whenever he could, and had her to thank for his own love of classical music. He didn't have the discipline to play music himself; he had been a Marine and learned his life lessons there. He knew in his bones that you never left someone you cared about to die alone.

Dan felt the girl watching him from her chair while she swung her legs. He covered the stump of his left arm, but gave her a quick smile, friendly without being encouraging. She didn't smile back.

"I can read," she said. She picked up the tablet and showed him the screen. It contained gibberish.

"I see," Dan said.

"100 and 100 is 200," she said proudly.

"That's very good."

She rolled her feet to make circles. "I'm really, really smart."

Dan nodded.

She pointed to the red cap he kept on the seat next to him.

"You're a Marine," she said.

"I was," Dan said. "How did you know? Are you a Marine?"

She shook her head and rolled her eyes. "I'm too little to be a Marine. I read your hat."

"Now I'm too old to be a Marine."

"Is your mother sick?" she asked.

"No," said Dan. "My sister."

"I thought it must be something like that. My mother is in this hospital. Again. We're here a lot. My grandmother and me. We don't have a father. Or a brother."

Before Dan could think of any response, the nurse and the grandmother returned. Both nodded thanks to Dan. The old woman took her granddaughter by the shoulder, and talked quietly to her.

"Let's go see your mother before we go home, Claire. Say thank you to the nice man and goodbye to him and the nurse."

She walked up to Dan, looking closely at his worn clothes, polished shoes, and one hand.

"I don't think you're a Marine," she said. "You only have one hand."

The grandmother gasped, but recovered with an embarrassed smile.

Dan squatted down so he could look at the girl face to face, and said, "Well, I don't think you're so smart."

Her nostrils flared, and she crossed her arms. With a toss of her golden head, keeping her chin high, she walked out without looking back.

As she left, the grandmother said, "Claire and I need to have a talk about manners and disability."

The nurse told Dan he could go back to see his sister if he wanted. As they walked to his sister's room the nurse huffed, "That wasn't very nice to say to that little girl."

"I know," Dan said. "I never know what to say to kids, you know?"

"Well, you've got to try harder than that."

The next day, Dan sat alone in the oppressive waiting room. He had lost track of the time, and suspected the nurses had probably forgotten that he was there. As a Marine, he had guarded water shipments for the planet's fragile hydration infrastructure. He had lost his hand four years ago fighting pirates trying to hijack a supply of precious water. He received disability benefits, rehabilitation and a prosthetic that was marvelously dextrous, but woefully insensate. Most days, Dan's biggest decision was whether to fasten the hand to the end of his arm, which gave people the illusion that he was whole. He usually chose to go without because it allowed him to feel the surfaces on which his arm rested.

He was about to search out a nurse when the little girl showed up. She looked deep into the mauve waiting area, saw Dan, but kept looking. She frowned when she saw that the complimentary basket of snacks was empty.

"Can I help you?" said Dan.

"No. I was looking for my friend Elise."

"Not here," he said.

She entered the waiting room and sat down on the same chair as yesterday. She didn't say anything, and she didn't swing her legs.

"Who is taking care of you?" asked Dan.

"Nobody." She swiveled her ankles in opposite directions, looking at her shoes. "But my grandma is here, too."

"Well, how are you, cutie?"

"I'm not a cutie," she said quickly.

"What are you?"

She thought for a while.

"A cupcake?" She giggled.

"Should I call you Cupcake, then?"

"Or Claire."

"You're the first Claire I've ever met. First girl named Cupcake, too."

Claire smiled.

"Did you eat all the cookies in the basket?" she asked.

"Nope. They were gone before I got here. Should we blame your friend Elise?"

She shrugged and then looked serious.

"My mother makes my grandma sad. But it's not her fault."

Dan looked up, hoping to see a nurse to pull him out of the conversation. They were alone though.

"My sister makes me sad, too," he said after a bit of silence.

"Everybody's worried about my mother. But I don't know what to do." She shook her golden hair. "What do you do for your sister?"

Dan blinked as he thought about an answer to a question no one had asked him. He cleared his throat, and began speaking slowly.

"Well, first, I hold her delicate hand. Sometimes that's all she needs is to know that someone is there with her."

"My mother holds my hand sometimes."

Dan waited, but Claire didn't add anything more.

"And I talk to her. I tell her stories about what we did when she and I were growing up. Sometimes I play the music that she likes."

"I don't know any music to play. All my songs are too silly or too happy to play for my mom."

"I know a song," he said. "It's a very pretty song. I bet you and your mom would like it."

She leaned forward a little. He balanced his cell phone in the crook of his left arm and looked in his classical music playlist. Under Debussy, he found "Claire de Lune."

"My sister played the violin in the Colonial Orchestra when this was recorded. Every time you hear it, you can remember it's the most beautiful song in the world. This music is named 'Claire.'"

She looked at him skeptically.

He played it for her, and she listened to the whole thing, her brow furrowed while she listened. When it was done, she nodded.

Dan downloaded the piece into her tablet, and showed her how to cue it up.

"I'm gonna to play it for my mother," she said. She ran from the waiting room.

Dan played the piece again. He had forgotten until then that his sister had helped create such a beautiful work of art. He was thankful Claire and her grandmother were not around to mock him for wasting tears.

A few days later, Dan saw Claire and her grandmother for the last time. It was a shock to see Claire's grandmother sobbing, who recognized Dan when he entered the waiting area. She shook her head, and he knew what they were dealing with. It was the same loss and grief that he would be facing shortly. He stood erect, but not too formally, and opened his arms. Claire's grandmother embraced him, and put her head on his shoulder while she cried.

To his surprise, Dan felt dampness on his shirt. He patted the older woman on her back. Tears for an original colonist were a luxury. He knew it was the last time he would see the woman or her granddaughter.

"I'm so sorry. I wish there was something I could do," he said. "Anything. I feel so useless."

"Claire plays that song you showed her all the time. It seemed to soothe my daughter. Thank you."

Claire came closer, but did not hug him. Dan held out his right hand, and she took it. Her hand felt like a porcelain locket, small and cool and closed tightly. After about a minute, Claire eased her hand away and left the waiting area. Dan helped her grandmother to sit, and then looked in the hallway to see where Claire had gone.

Near the end of the hall, he saw Claire hand in hand with another little girl with a tangle of dark, untamed curls. They walked up to him.

"This is my friend Elise. Do you know her?"

Dan squatted down to be face level with both of them. He extended his hand to shake Elise's hand. She pulled away.

"It's okay," said Claire. "He's only got one hand because he's disabled." Claire took Dan's hand, and joined it to Elise's.

"She's pretty sad because her dad's in here. I thought she should meet you. She's not as smart as me, though. Right?"

Elise shrugged with embarrassment, and looked at Dan, her dark eyes sorrowful in a wan face.

Dan shook Elise's hand. Then he leaned closer to Claire.

"You're rotten," he said.

Claire smiled defiantly. Then, facing her friend, she said, "He was a Marine. He knows all the beautiful songs in the world."

The dark-haired girl looked at Dan, trying to understand what that meant.

Claire stepped in to help. She looked at Dan and asked, "Do you think there might be a song just for her?"

Dan saw a hopeful look in Elise's face. He thought about his classical playlist for only a moment before saying, "There just might be something." He chose a sonata by Beethoven. While it played, he saw wonder in the dark-haired girl's face, and a slight smile on Claire's lips.

Before the sonata ended, Claire put her small, tender hand on two of his artificial fingers, and closed her porcelain locket hand tightly.

Digital Footprint

Tanasha Martin

I greet the dawn in a place unknown.
A mirrored image, a lone touchstone.
And it's clearly shown,
it's unequivocally my own.

No matter how long or intense the stare,
no recognition will blare
or seems to register there.
Is it too soon for despair?

Shades of brown, hair and eyes.
Each surface that may rise,
displays reflections of silent lies.
No one's there to hear my cries.

A surge of panic lights my heart.
No memory of self to compart.
Each attempt picks me apart.
Where on earth should I start?

Silence writhes, its grip is tight.
Has the me inside taken flight?
That part of me, as dark as night.
I crave assurance I'll be alright.

My cell phone screen's a mirror, black.
A busy landline signals back.
Natural disaster, terror attack?
How else could I react?

Through a catacomb of empty rooms
My search for evidence resumes.
In a nightmare that consumes
Terror seeds and blooms.

News reports: An emergency transmission
Sent around the world, waves to our cognition,
a permanent condition?
Everyone? In the same position?

Instructions: Remain at home, a safety zone
Until the culprits are shown
and the cure is known.
I am on my own.

The wave that stole me from my mind
Has left fear and frustration behind
So I'm flying blind.
Walls close in, confine.

My pulse pounds, breathing is hard.
What to focus on or disregard?
Cracked window? Credit card?
An empty yard?

I can't rest until I've tried.
I dare to risk a step outside
And hope to decide
My hysteria's unjustified.

Every soul I dare approach
mimics a fearful, desperate reproach.
Should I continue to encroach
with no information to poach?

They rage, riot, scream and cry,
For loss they can't identify.
Under a crystal blue, dry
still suburban sky.

Sense of self, a shared loss.
The burden of this albatross.
Little desire for unity across
the widespread chaos.

I sprint to "home", engage bolt and chain
Wrack my shaken, addled brain
To attempt to ascertain,
what clues remain.

I continue my search, in closet and drawer
and find a cherished photo store.
I'd missed them before.
Could there be more?

Papers and names in files and then,
a passport photo, a twin
of who I've previously been.
Familiar, yet foreign skin.

I fear to venture beyond this street.
My empty persona, hollow, obsolete.
Out there, they're also incomplete,
The consolation, bittersweet.

I sleep with lights to chase the dark.
Wake with a pounding chest, the brightness stark—
a solitary idea spark:
I must've left a media mark...

I scramble to the desk, for laptop and chair,
A password is an answered prayer.
And attempt every icon there,
Photos of me — everywhere.

On social media, several sites,
Evidence my cruelty and spite.
Verbal sparring, my words indict.
My God, this can't be *right*.

Pictures posted, casually
Are now publicly, irrevocably,
the only image of me.
Is *that* who I want to be?

The only thing I can control, my decision —
to change the harshness and derision,
is to enter with calculated precision,
more considerate word incision.

To broadcast kindness to strangers, friends,
ideas and language that transcends.
I'll erase what hurts and offends
and try to make amends.

I take my seat, and set to type
away each grieved, vindictive snipe.
And commit to obliterate, to wipe
away every single gripe.

Delete the cause of my depth of shame.
Cleanse the slate and accept the blame,
this self-imposed defame,
of my good name.

To use persistence and ingenuity,
during this time of ambiguity,
and recreate ME —
My singular opportunity.

To impress upon the world, represent
the nature I want, no, *need* to re-invent.
A guide, a blueprint
to a better digital footprint.

Solace

Sara Vallejo

Nora is unflagging in her determination. I wish I could say I felt the same. I fear our mission was doomed from the start, but there is no one I would rather have stolen away into the dark with. Love does not make us blind. I knew we would crawl through the sheeting rain and muck, through the unrelenting dark, never to see our friends and family again. Never to see the light of the sun. When Nora's gran died, so too did the last colonist who had ever felt the warmth of the sunlight on her skin. How the light went out of my love's steely eyes that day, how she pounded the galvanized steel walls of our bunk until her fists were red and raw. How she howled curses into the cacophony of the storm raging just beyond our door, until she had no voice left. Still the thunder cracked and the lightning split the ever-dark sky.

The pain lancing through me is nothing compared to what she suffered. I duck my head against the rain, water slicking off my tactical jacket. A few steps ahead of me, Colonel Fitzhugh raises his hand to shield his eyes against the rain and shines his flashlight on his nav, shaking his head.

"Fitz?" Nora calls, and I'm grateful that she jogs ahead to meet him. I allow the grimace of pain I've been hiding from her all day. They exchange words and Nora runs a shaking hand through her short, dripping hair. It's bad news, I know. Fitzhugh told me, his voice low, that the storms buggered his nav systems. Forget GPS. The electric storms make connecting to the satellites that our forebears had launched into orbit around our sad, shivering exoplanet all but impossible. No one has heard from Earth since we'd settled. Earth hasn't heard from us. "They've written us off," Nora growled one night, shaken from sleep by night terrors. Sweat had plastered her dishwater blond hair to her forehead and she had paced our small room until her trembling subsided. No rescue mission was coming and none of us truly expected one, but there was always that damnable glimmer of hope. No longer. "We have to do something, Iyari. Anything, god."

So we had. Just five of us, trying to find the terraforming engine that had thrown our world into storms instead of seeding it with life. Our colony will not survive if we cannot fix the terraforming engine. Our world will dwindle, a flickering light in the dark, until we are overtaken, extinguished by unending storms.

The colonel is the only one of us with survival experience, the only one who has been out in the squall that batters our settlement. Like me, he doesn't expect to return to New Arcadia. He'll join all of those he sent to their deaths, all on missions just like ours. There hasn't been a mission in half a decade. Nora and I hadn't yet reached our majority then, barely younger than Katya is now. Katya, a geologist who paints a picture of what our world could be in mineral samples of glittering mica, buff-colored limestone, dark and cloudy quartz. Katya, no more than a slip of a girl, shouldering a pack nearly half her size, because she aches to see the sun cresting over the rugged mountains she's only ever seen in topographical surveys.

They are the dreamers, Katya, and Nora, and Nazim. Nora, the horticultural engineer who coaxes food from grow labs instead of soil. Naz who teaches the children of New Arcadia to read and write, younger than I am but already expecting his first child. We have children young in New Arcadia, to populate this barren rock we're trapped on. If only we'll be able to feed them. Life is scarce without sunlight.

Boots splash and he trots up beside me. Naz is dark, like I am. As we made camp one night, he told me our skin was dark because our ancestors had come from lands bathed in sunlight. I can't imagine such places. "You're limping."

I force a bright, toothy grin, through every step is agony. "My blisters have blisters. On the plus side, I think trudging through mud is doing wonders for my backside."

"Your backside *is* a wonder."

"You're lucky Carrie's not here to catch you saying things like that."

Naz's easy smile disappears. "I miss her. Like crazy. When do you suppose we'll get back to New Arcadia?"

Naz is the only one of us who truly believes we'll make it back to our settlement. Even Katya voiced her doubts to me, standing over my shoulder as she showed me the mineral samples she collected that day. We'd been just days outside of New Arcadia then, and already she knew. But Naz, Naz believes in us, in New Arcadia. In sunlight. It's why we should never have let him come on our expedition. It's why I'm so glad we did. "In time for the little one, I'm sure. Carrie'd have my head if I let you miss it." When we left, Carrie was already round with their child. "Another week or two and I won't be able to see my feet," she'd whined, but still she smiled.

A flash of something passes through his dark eyes and he sobers. "I'm doing it for her. My daughter."

I smile. "I know." Better this, dying trying to bring life and vitality to our world, than to watch her starve when another green room goes down as one by one our grow lights reach critical failure.

I'm doing this for Nora.

We make camp in a rocky crevasse. It's a rough climb down, but the rocks provide some shelter from the downpour. I pitch our tent, my movements stiff, as Nora and Colonel Fitzhugh frown over his nav. She climbs a few long steps back up the rock and nods down to him. She squints against the rain and smiles. I'm too far away to see it, but I know her smile in the way she ducks her head, the way her shoulders round.

Katya breaks my reverie. She's the youngest among us, and sweet like

Naz. Her every expression is telegraphed larger than life on her round face.

"I know I said I wanted to do a geological study so that after we find the terraforming engine and get our planet, you know, less soggy, we would know where and what to build. But right now, I don't give a damn. The only thing I want is dry pants." She rolls her glittering brown eyes, rain drops spiking her eyelashes.

"A warm bed."

"Ooh," she croons, as she favors me with a lascivious smile. "A hot meal."

"A shower."

We look up into the downpour and laugh. She tosses me two packs of rations and ducks into her small, one-man tent, letting the flap fall shut behind her. Her task lights are on in seconds and I see her silhouetted against the nylon, huddled over the pack she's fashioned into a makeshift worktable. When fiery pain woke me from sleep the night before, my bloodied toes curling in my boots, her lights had still been on, a warm distant glow. She will be the first of us to wake in the morning, the last of us to sleep as she crumbles sandy soil samples between her fingertips.

Nora jogs down the crevasse and into my arms. She crushes the rations between us, the mylar crinkling. For a moment, the cold and damp are gone, and there is only this, her lips curving in a smile against my cheek, her forehead against mine. She kisses me sweetly and takes the rations from me and holds open the flap to our tent, offering me in with a smile I know is just for me.

We eat and then strip off our wettest gear, hanging it from tent poles to dry. Nothing is ever dry out here. Brown-red blood stains my socks, so I quickly shove my feet back in my boots before Nora can see. She's flicking through her tablet, scrolling through lines and lines of data. That's how it all began, with data. Searching the lines and lines of code for just what went wrong. "It has to be the range," she mutters. "A figure must be off somewhere or something..."

I sigh and lie down alongside her. She sets the tablet aside and slings an arm low over my hip. She buries her face in the crook of my neck and her short hair is cool and slick against my skin. "I hope sunshine feels like this," she murmurs, and it's not long before her breath deepens and slows. Sleep doesn't come to me for hours.

Our camp is shaken awake by thunder that moves the very earth beneath us. We scramble to pack our gear as the rain courses into the crevasse. We are just cresting the top when the ground beneath us starts to move. It happens so quickly. Katya is handing her pack up to me so she can find purchase as stones skitter beneath her feet. Her hand slips from the strap and the earth slips beneath her. I grab for her hand as her boots sink into the streaming mud and torrents of rain.

"Iyari!" she shouts, my name swallowed up by the storm. Naz races to the crevasse's edge, but Colonel Fitzhugh pushes him back, crossing to us and grabbing Katya's arm.

Her eyes are round with terror, flashing back the lightning that splits the sky. She is torn from us in an instant, and we nearly follow. Naz grabs my pack and yanks me back. I fall hard on my ass, but I'm out of harm's way. He pulls the colonel away from the edge, away from the sliding earth. Their heated shouts are drowned out up by the roar of the landslide, and the colonel only relents, falling to his knees, when the safety beacon on Katya's jacket disappears into the punishing, sifting mud. We are no use to New Arcadia if the earth claims us as well.

Naz and Nora say a prayer. The colonel clips us all to a length of paracord. I see Katya's face, tears and rain swimming in the corners of her wide eyes. We carry on in silence.

I am stumbling by midday, every step burning. I feel Naz's hand on my back and I clutch his arm for support as we trudge onward. Our eyes meet and he catches me as I sag, but my vision is indistinct. Nora turns when she feels the tug of the paracord and Katya's terror-filled eyes are alive again in Nora's alarm. She's kneeling in the muck beside me before I can try to stagger to my feet. Her hands are cool on my heated face and she shouts something to the colonel. She shines a light in my eyes and I squint against it but she forces my eyes open. Her pale face swims before my eyes and then the earth slips away beneath me. Is this how Katya felt when she was carried away? No. I feel light, a wisp of smoke as the heat kindles inside me. This, I think, is what sunlight must feel like. Heat. Blistering, unforgiving agony.

Everything around me is light. Even the ever-dark sky has lightened, gray and green like a week-old bruise. I reach for it and then fall away, back into the dark.

Voices rumble around me like thunder. I feel fingertips—Nora's—on my lips and then bitterness floods my mouth. I struggle, try to cough and spit it out, but Nora covers my mouth with her hand and pleads in a broken voice until I've swallowed all of the bitter powder. She takes my hand in both of hers and her skin is so cold. I am blazing like the sun. She is as cool as rain. I must be smoke, because I float, disconnected from the burning pain, the damp, tethered to the world only by Nora's desperate grasp.

"I should have... Her fever..."

"You're not a doctor, Nora." Naz.

"I'm not anything. I'm not a doctor or a terraform engineer. I'm not an expeditioner."

The deeper rumble must be the colonel. "I've seen it before. 'Trench foot' they used to call it. I should have..."

Nora is crying, tears as hot as my skin, as she presses our clasped hands to her face.

The colonel's deep rumble. "She needs to rest."

Then Naz, squeezing my other hand. "They both do."

They drift away and light crashes against my eyelids like waves. Light like I've never seen before.

"I'm not crazy, right? The light, it's..." There is something in Naz's voice that I haven't heard in years. Something so powerful it cuts through the smoke and the heat inside me. Hope.

I wake with Nora curled around me. The heat inside me is gone and when I open my eyes, I see first the tracks tears have traced down her cheeks and then, then the light that struck awe into Naz's voice. I am still for a moment, sinking back into my body. The pain is there, but lessened. Nora's arm is a comforting weight around me, warm and sweet. Yet, even if I close my eyes, I can't imagine us back at the settlement, tangled together in our bunk, for there is no ever-present growl of thunder punctuating this bliss.

For a heart-stopping moment, I wonder if this is the beautiful dream I'll dream as I fall forever into the dark. But then Nora murmurs, "Hey," in a creaky, broken voice. The voice of a woman who's been crying and praying in her every waking moment. The voice, even as it breaks, more precious to me than any other.

"Did we find it?"

"We're close," she whispers, a promise. Close to the machine that wrecked our world, the machine that can right it. Even here, the storms have quieted. "I can fix it."

"You figured it out?"

She helps me sit and presses her canteen to my lips. "I think so. I think the range is misconfigured. Just a typo. A missed zero and the algorithm broke. Katya'd know better but..." Her words are halting, unsure. "It's lighter here, Iyari. There's... there's sun trying to break through the cloud cover. If i'm right, the terraforming engine is working just fine, but it's not projecting the right range. If we fix that, then..."

She doesn't have to put words to the hope burgeoning inside me. I see what our world could be. Naz and Carrie teaching their daughter to walk in grass that tickles her toes. Nora, digging her fingers into loamy soil as she coaxes little green shoots to push through the earth to meet the sun. "Then we have to go. What are we waiting for?"

Nora hugs me close. "You need to rest. The infection... Why didn't you tell me you were so torn up?"

I close my eyes and shake my head. I have no answer for her. Maybe love *is* blinding. Blinding like the sun that's just starting to filter through the blanketing of storm clouds. It makes me stupid and stubborn and hopeful.

We break camp just two days later, though Nora still frets over me. I take her hand and let her guide me, support me. She warms me from my very core.

As the sky lightens, the horizon heaves toward the heavens. The colonel traces a range of mountains on his topographical map. The Archimedes Mountains. I take the map from him and brace it on Nora's shoulders. I cross out the label in china crayon and Nora snickers at the sensation. In wobbly letters, I write in their new name. Sierra Katya.

With every step, we walk into a new world, a world none of us has ever known. We walk on soft, springy clover and creeping Charlie, seeded by drones from the terraforming engine. I don't know what is more glorious, the verdant green, our Eden, or the awe that lights in Nora's eyes, her breathless exhilaration as she lets her fingers trail through tall, tickling prairie grasses.

"I've never seen anything so beautiful," she murmurs.

Neither have I.

The sky is a blue so pure that every other shade I've seen before is undeserving of the name. The sunlight on my skin feels just like Nora wished it would. We make it to the terraforming engine when the sun is high in the sky. It towers over us, a gleaming monolith of metal. Nora is at the control panel in an instant, looking between the data stream on her tablet and the engine's monitor. She types in a few lines of code, a rudimentary patch until we can get an engineer out here.

She spends hours tapping at the keyboard, looking back and forth between the display and her tablet. Her smile grows with every keystroke. Naz and I pick wildflowers and weave them into careful crowns. For Carrie and their baby girl. For Katya.

We leave the colonel to his surveying and venture into the hills at the base of the mountains. We find a quiet brooklet tucked away, carving its way through stone. It is unlike anything we've ever seen before. Even old photographs of Earth pale to the world unfurling before us. Naz kneels, presses his forehead to the soft sand at the banks of the brook and says a prayer for Katya. We make a tower out of the most beautiful stones we can find and place her flower crown atop it.

Nora's shout draws us out of our reverie, out of the hills. She's calling my name, her voice triumphant, and Naz and I break into a run, stumbling and laughing. We reach the terraforming engine breathless, beaming, clutching at the stitches in our sides.

She takes my hands and draws me close. "Iyari. Iyari, listen."

A hesitant voice crackles through the comm.

«New Arcadia settlement to Solace Expedition. Solace, do you read?»

My Tita Elena. Her voice is hesitant. The very first communication sent across our new home world. The patch must have tempered the storms enough for the satellites to transmit.

Another voice cuts in. «You're supposed to say 'over' when you're done.» My cousin. I can imagine my aunt pinching him by the ear and sure enough, a second later. «Ow, quit it! ...Over.»

My heart in my throat, I punch a button on the comms. "Tita?"

Is it her muffled sob that sounds over the comm or my own?

«You've done it. You've...»

«Hey, Ma. Don't cry, hey?»

I cling to Nora, shaking with each sob.

«Sit tight, angel,» My aunt says. «Help is on the way.»

«But then Ma's gonna smack you one for sneaking off. What? Ow! It's not like you saved the planet or—hey!»

Our sobs turn to laughter and the sun dries our tears.

That night we camp under the stars and I don't know what is more beautiful,
the light of day or this clear night. We stay awake, taking in the beauty of the night,
of the dawn. Nora leans against me, and I press a kiss to her cheek and lace my fingers with hers.

"We did it," I whisper.

We watch the sun rise on a brand new day.

Playback

Elaine Fisher

The thick fog that rolled in from the bay each morning dissipated by the time Harold took his daily walk to the mailbox house. He breathed in the salty ocean air and shuffled along the wooden planks. Everyone in the houseboat community recognized the elderly man who always had his Canon DSLR around his neck. He tried to recall their names and start a greeting, but stopped midstream. Only the name 'Catherine' stuck in his mind. The image of her sparkling green eyes filled his eyes with their brightness. He looked at his neighbors with a lopsided smile, shrugged his shoulders, and continued on his walk.

"Maybe it will arrive today," Harold confided to his camera.

He finally approached the mailbox house that sat on a weathered pier post. The house was a large wooden box painted white with three shelves, three rural mailboxes for each shelf, a total of nine. Only the doors of the mailboxes showed, each painted a different color.

"You are perfect...it's the Rule of Thirds."

He positioned himself so that each mailbox lined up along the grids in his viewfinder. Affectionately cradling his camera firmly in his hands, he whispered, "Ready now...won't shake ya, shutter speed just right."

This was one of his favorite shots, but most of the time he forgot he already had taken it. Later when he reviewed his pictures, he deleted a half-dozen identical shots.

Harold opened the blue hinged-door and peered inside. He searched with arthritic fingers that quivered with anticipation.

"It's finally here."

Harold snatched a padded envelope out from the blue mailbox and it nearly slipped from his grasp. He walked to a nearby bench, carefully opened the envelope — a memory card, lens, and adaptor slid out. Also included was a shiny sheet of paper with an unusual drawing of a camera lens that looked like a human eye. This striking image filled him with wonder and hope as he scanned down the sheet to read the following instructions:

Photographic Memory from PHOTO MAGIC— if you can see it, you can relive it.

1. Replace old memory card with new Photo Magic memory card. Allows the mind to play back memories in unforgettable detail.

2. Replace old lens with 3D vision lens for a natural immersion into past images.

3. Place adapter on viewfinder and then press red button to activate Photo Magic - the latest in mind-eye technology that imprints past memories on the new card.

4. Navigate your past with your camera's Playback Arrow. Photo Magic accessories are compatible with most DSLR cameras. Now you're ready to go back as far as your eye can see.

Harold stared at the new accessories and whispered, "New things frighten me. I'm not ready yet to try them out. But I really want to... go back... home." Whenever he thought of home, his mind snapped a picture of Catherine beckoning him to return.

He compared his memory to film photography because his mind sometimes felt like a dark room where the pictures could be over or underexposed. If only he could find his missing, perfectly developed photographs from years ago, he wouldn't feel so lost. His life lately looked like a photograph of a dull, blurry landscape with him standing far in the distance, all alone.

After stuffing the camera accessories into his camera bag, Harold stood up from the bench. The warm ocean breeze ruffled his gray hair as he walked along the pier back to his houseboat. He continued taking pictures along the way, looking for good composition and good lighting, especially practicing his skills on his favorite houseboat, the lovely little white one with ceramic flowerpots filled with red geraniums.

As a photographer, he especially paid attention to color. Red and white suddenly triggered a glimpse from his past—Catherine holding red roses from their garden, standing in front of their freshly painted white home. A perfect shot...snap! His eyes lit up as he captured the memory, but it was a fleeting moment replaced by a familiar darkness that filled his mind. Then his wife and their home disappeared as he returned to the present.

He approached the next houseboat. The striking colors of yellow and blue with a painted giant purple seahorse on its side encouraged him to bring the viewfinder back up to his eye. He hoped the people who lived there were as happy as the place looked.

Again, he struggled for another glimpse of Catherine, her welcoming arms outstretched, and her black wind-blown hair suspended in time. His eyes welled up as he tried in vain to relive in his mind the happy times they had together.

After a few more houseboats, his dark gray houseboat appeared. Snap ... he captured the picture, then pointed his camera upward and caught the crying seagulls swooping overhead. These were great photos but this place would never feel like "home" to him. He quickly deleted the images from his camera's playback. If only his mind could delete his loneliness as easily.

Out of the corner of his eye, seemingly out of nowhere, a black cat crossed his path, giving him a long stare as Harold gazed into sparkling green eyes. What was usually a bad omen filled him with hope.

He quickly snapped a shot as the cat gracefully maneuvered a leap to the pier's railing, levitating in mid-air — like magic.

"Oh, lovely Cat!" Harold crooned, remembering he sometimes called his wife that name.

He walked to his houseboat with a little pep to his stride. Once inside, he sat on his rocker looking out at the water, his camera in his lap, and took the new accessories from his bag. The instructions assured him that his mind was like a camera, memories stored, nothing really forgotten. He inserted the new memory card and replaced the lens with the new 3D lens. Attaching the adapter to the viewfinder, he raised the camera to his eye, and then pressed the red button.

He focused on the past, impatiently tapping the playback arrow until she appeared — like magic.

"Catherine, you're really here!" Harold smiled at his wife.

His eyes opened wide to let in the light.

Lost on the South Lawn

Annerose Walz

It's exactly how I imagined the last seconds before dying. My life flashes in front of my eyes, scenes from graduation, soccer practice, my grandfather reading to me, my first steps ... then, a tunnel with a bright light at the end. Cold creeps into my bones, and dizziness floods over me as I drift into total nothingness and absolute silence.

Oh, I'm not dying, although it might seem like it. I, Jersey Prexton, am time traveling. For the first time in my life and probably the last.

Slithering through darkness and time, I don't feel the tightness of the Flynhard Capsule anymore. It's like floating in the Dead Sea. I close my eyes. Besides the little green flashing dot on the screen in front of me, there is nothing to see anyway.

What a feeling.

"Hey, Jexton! I just saw you in kindergarten with your blond corkscrew curls..." Elroy's grating voice ruins the moment I have dreamed of my whole life.

Urgh, of course, he can never keep his mouth shut.

"KIM: Elroy, no talking during hyper-spiraling!" the third crew member in the capsule sends a flashing message to our dashboards from her back seat.

Miss Overachiever, always playing by the rules. I roll my eyes and wonder for the umpteenth time why I had to end up with these two, of all people.

We are the three best of the 15,757 students in our high school history class. Mr. Flynhard, founder and owner of the legendary *Fly Past Company*, who started the Time Travel program 75 years ago, sponsored this time travel jump as our Excellence Award. It's our challenge, too. The one who presents the best research results after coming back will gain a position in Flynhard's company. The chance of a lifetime.

Flynhard let us choose any place and time we wanted, except the years between 2018 and 2040. They are still sealed.

After long discussions, we chose one of the last mysteries of history, November 22nd, 1963.

This might be the only chance I have to time travel. Technically, time travel is not a big deal anymore. It is reserved for the shrinks and the history professors. Time Travel uses too many of our precious resources. Nobody travels just for the fun of it the way they did back in the early 22nd century.

Now, in 2154, we only travel for research, and it's restricted to observations. No interactions.

"Whoa!" Elroy says. "Jexton, see the lights?"

The moment I open my eyes, a shock wave runs over us and throws me against the side of the capsule. Lights with different colors flash all over my dashboard. The loud scratching noises send currents through me. The lights stop.

"What's going on? Kim?" We've been trained to fly the capsule, but this is nothing I've ever seen. It usually operates on autopilot, except for emergencies. I'm trained to be the pilot, Elroy the navigator, and Kim our data collector.

"I don't know, it's... weird." Kim's voice sounds concerned. As the science nerd, she usually keeps her cool, she never uses simple words like *weird*. Kim is the logical thinker; I'm the intuitive planner. And Elroy, well, he is his own category. The always-talking-bragging-and-dreadlock-swinging category - in short, a pain in the neck. But he is also an excellent navigator and as our Naval Flight Officer, he is in charge of the SMT weapon.

My monitor is down, there's not even a green flashing dot. Another shock wave churns us even more. I feel the capsule twirling.

"Elroy, what's the T-GPS status?" I hear him flip some switches.

The Time and Geolocation Positioning System should tell us where we are, time-wise as well as in space.

"Sorry, Jex, I got nothing," he states and adds, "well, beside the little Black Widow on my screen, her red hourglass is spinning."

He's obsessed with Marvel, but even though he is joking, I can hear the edge in his voice.

Shoot! What is happening?

I'm pressed into my seat when the capsule comes to an abrupt halt.

"The security protocol has kicked in," Kim states.

The capsule is programmed to slow down just before it is about to crash into something. It's an automatic brake. I feel the downward drift. The landing is just a slight bump.

I flip some switches. Nothing. My monitor stays pitch black.

"Whoa, whoa... that's not possible," Elroy says.

"What's wrong?"

"Oh snap! Jex, everything is wrong! We landed in 2036."

"The capsule malfunctioned. The time seal-lock is broken," Kim reports.

This is bad, really bad. The years between 2018 and 2040 are sealed, most of the files destroyed. Nobody is allowed to travel to this time period. Ever. It is called the *11th-hour period*, the time when humanity almost destroyed itself and the Earth - drastic climate change, wars, and deadly diseases raged everywhere. Everybody cared only about themselves.

Only three teams of history professors traveled to the 11th-hour period. They all returned in various stages of mental breakdown. When these professors came back, some exited the capsule and killed everyone in their vicinity, or they sat in the capsule and didn't speak another word. Ever. Others got out and dropped dead. The survivors are held in a mental health facility near Futura-City-One.

I should know. My grandfather is one of them. He doesn't speak, but he wrote me some letters. The content was so disturbing that my parents threw the letters away. I rescued them from the garbage bin and hid them. That's how I know how time travel feels. Grandpa also painted dystopian visions of the cold heartlessness of people who almost destroyed this planet and asteroids that exploded into the moon.

One letter ended with *accepting diversity could overcome the angst.* Words, that I have been mulling over and over ever since.

After the last of these three time travel teams came back, all the governments and tribes of the Earth decided to seal those years so that nobody would go there again. Our leaders did this for our protection. There should never be another 11th-hour period.

Capsules are now equipped with a time seal-lock to avoid someone ending up accidentally in the forbidden time zone.

There are lots of rumors about this period, but in general, we are not allowed to speak about it.

I sometimes wonder if not knowing is really protecting us. And if it was such a bad time, why are we still here?

Guess we are about to find out.

The blinds of the capsule's windows slowly lower, revealing a limited view. Smoke is everywhere. Through the fog, I see patches of grass on the ground.

"You're not gonna like this, Jex!"

"Elroy, I'm in no mood for jokes. What is it?"

"We landed in the South Lawn Fountain," he chuckles.

What South Lawn? Does he mean the old White House South Lawn? That can't be ... "Come on, don't be such an idiot."

"What? It's true."

"Give me the T-GPS so I can verify what you are babbling." Kim is on edge, too.

Elroy rattles out the numbers, "2036.04.12T 38°53'46.1"N 77°02'11.7"W"

"His statement is correct. We are sitting in the middle of the South

Lawn Fountain, in front of the White House in Washington, DC."

How did that happen?

Soldiers emerge from the smoke, running towards our capsule, their guns point at us. I'm sure they have no clue what they are dealing with.

"Sheesh, Jexton, any suggestions? We gotta go." Elroy's voice screams in my ears.

"I tried. Battery doesn't start. We are stuck."

So much to no interactions.

Since Kim sits in the back, she is the first to exit.

"Chinese!" Shouts and screams erupt around us. More and more people come into sight, some with notepads, some with cameras. Everybody is staring at Kim.

Snapping pictures, a woman shouts, "Oh my gosh, are these aliens?"

"No, Chinese! Told you, they're coming for us, with their new weapon ..." the journalist at her side shouts and pulls her away from us - at least he tries.

"Jexton, do something before they shoot her," Elroy whispers behind me.

"Excuse me," my voice sounds cold and metallic over the outboard loudspeaker. "We are not Chinese, we do not have any weapons, and we are not here to harm you."

"Get out of that thing. Now!" A soldier stands right in front of my small window outlet and barks into a cone shaped device, I recognize as an old-fashioned bullhorn.

"Okay, we will... just don't shoot us. We come in peace."

Elroy chuckles. "Sheesh, you sound like a drunk B-movie actor, Jex."

"Elroy. Just. Get. Out."

He is so annoying.

I push the button for automatic battery loading.

My breath catches in my throat when I climb out and look at where I expect the White House to be. A huge crater is gaping at me. The whole building is gone. I shake my head. Elroy and Kim are staring at the big hole with the same horror on their faces. Three men hurry over and handcuff us. Others pull yellow tape around the capsule and send the reporters off.

"What happened here?" I ask one of the men. He clenches his teeth.

They half push, half pull us towards a building to the west. Elroy asks question after question. His guard is tight-lipped, too.

They lock us in a cold bunker somewhere underground.

"What do you think happened here? I mean, it looks as if a dinosaur devoured the president's residence for breakfast. Do you think it was the Chinese?" Elroy asks.

"Don't know, but it looks like a war zone, something that just happened" I shrug. "I mean, we knew that the White House was destroyed, but ..."

"The crater is about 172.5 feet long and 154.8 feet wide. The White House had 132 rooms, including 16 family-guest rooms, 3 kitchens and 35 bathrooms. All gone. That was a huge detonation. Did any of you turn around and check if the Washington Monument was still there? I estimate it is gone, too, calculating the force that was needed to erase the White House."

I stare at Kim. *I have no clue how she knows things like that.* We all have different coping mechanisms, I suppose.

The metal door is flung open. A heavy-set man walks in. His uniform and military haircut speak volumes. Four soldiers stomp in behind him. *Five-star general. Wow, they grace us with the big shot.*

"Who are you?" He addresses Kim.

Kim gets up and starts, "My name is Kim StJohn, this is Jersey Prexton, and..."

"Sit down! How did you get on the South Lawn? Who sent you?"

"That's quite rude, General," Elroy interrupts him. "She was about to introduce me too. I'm Elroy Brody, from the famous Brody Family in New York." He extends his right hand, still cuffed to the left. "And your name, Sir?"

I roll my eyes. *Of course, he would play the rich-boy card.*

The general eyes Elroy like an annoying insect.

He abruptly slams his fists on the table and leans close to Kim's face. She doesn't flinch.

"How did you get through air ban security? This is a war zone. We are practically at war with you, the People's Republic of China."

Elroy leans close. "Excuse me, Sir, Kim is not Chinese. We told you that. By the way, wouldn't it be stupid to land somewhere close, if we would've caused this? Why would we do that? To make sure we hit the jackpot?"

The general glances at Elroy and shouts, "In the middle of global negotiations about what we're going to do about this darn asteroid, the Chinese secretly try to shoot it from its orbit, miss, and accidentally pulverize the White House? They denied it immediately. But who else could've done it? Then you show up ... So, do you really think I believe you have nothing to do with this?"

Elroy's hand flies to his weapon. I search for his eyes, press my lips together and shake my head slightly. *Don't do anything stupid. I'm glad they didn't recognize it as a weapon when they searched us.*

Elroy furrows his eyebrows and stares at the general's name tag.

He exclaims, "Are you THE General McKinney? The famous A.S. McKinney, with A standing for Arthur and S for Shoppenhauer?" With each word, his voice grows more enthusiastic. "The one they named the asteroid after?"

The general pinches his eyebrows even further and pierces his eyes in Elroy.

"Yes, I am McKinney, but the asteroid is named 2004 MN4."

"Asteroid 2004 MN4 was discovered in 2004. A collision with Earth was theoretically possible on April 13, 2029 or April 13, 2036." Kim says. "Unfortunately, we have no record of what really happened, only that the asteroid was renamed after the General that helped to prevent its collision with our moon. It still circles the Earth."

What is she doing? She can't just share this information. We don't even know how this will effect our own time.

The general jerks back, turns and points to the door. "Everybody out! Now!"

The soldiers only hesitate a tenth of a second.

The general takes a deep breath. "What kind of clowns are you? How did you get this confidential information? Nobody knows about the moon yet - we just found out and communications are down."

When I see Elroy open his mouth, I decide to take the lead. This is way too sensitive to let him talk.

"General McKinney, we are American citizens."

"Kind of," Elroy mumbles. Technically, we are not citizens, but the fact that we have other kinds of governments where we come from is irrelevant.

"Listen." I stare at the general to fix his gaze on me. "We are here to help." Another lie. If everything had gone according to plan, we would be watching J. F. Kennedy's motorcade cruising through downtown Dallas to investigate his assassination.

"We can help you nudge this asteroid from its orbit," Kim offers.

"Why should I trust you?" McKinney points a finger at her.

"Just because I look Chinese doesn't mean that's all I am, General." Kim's voice is sharp, her eyes hard.

"She's American, I vouch for her," Elroy throws in.

"There are three options to deflect an asteroid. Pushing it off course through a gravitational tractor, changing its orbital motion through the impact of an object and the nuclear bomb method," Kim states, "but none of these will work in the short period of time you have left."

"I'm listening."

"The best solution would be to push it away with an enormous kinetic magnetic field, which can be produced by slightly changing the function of the new XL Hadron Collider they are building under the North Pole and connect it with all orbiting satellites. This would produce a kinetic-magnetic shield around the moon, like a rippling security wave that pushes the asteroid away. You would need the cooperation of the space operating agencies of all nations and the agreement of all governments. Going united is essential."

"How old are you? You look like a junior high student," the general says. "Don't they use the LHC to collide particles?"

"I'm eighteen years old and was the best in all my high school classes, not only in mathematics, astrophysics, chemistry, but also in world history, social economy, psychology, and war strategy. The original LHC was built to collide particles, but when you change its working process, you could bundle the particles. It's complicated but if you let me speak to some astrophysicists? Please?"

I hope Kim knows what she is doing. Out time is running out. We have only three hours left to get back into our capsule. A retracting omega ray will collect us back to the future; the only rescue option we have, in case the battery is not charging.

"General, there's a lot of chaos right now, this world is at the edge of a new world war. All the diverse populations fight against each other. Not working together over frontiers, cultures, races, religions, ages, and other divides will almost destroy this planet - but it doesn't. There is still hope. This is your chance, no country can solve this issue alone, and if you take charge, and convince your President to make a difference you all will save the Earth," I say, raising my eyebrows.

Silence spreads between us.

"I would suggest you don't waste any more time, Sir," I add. "We only have three hours."

"Nonsense!" The general stomps out.

Fifteen minutes pass before a group of white coats walk in. Our cuffs are taken off and Kim explains her strategy to the scientists.

Then the metal door shuts behind the mumbling scientists.

"Hey, you cannot just leave us here!" I protest.

"Urgh, of course, they can." Elroy bumps his fist on the door. "Now what?"

"We have to get outta here," I sigh, and look at him. "Well, pull your

SMTW and do your magic."

"Yes!" A smile spreads on his face.

I would have preferred not to have to use the weapon.

We insert our special earplugs. Elroy pulls a necklace out of his shirt. The small multi-tool weapon looks like a whistle. Ten seconds after he starts to work the door, it springs open. He peeks outside and signs us to follow. Nobody is in the hallway, but there are voices ahead.

Elroy blows the whistle. An instant later, we walk around the corner. Three guards lie writhing on the ground, their hands over their ears. Our new weapons are quite effective and non-lethal. Elroy uses the necklace whenever someone gets in our way, while Kim leads us back through the underground hallways. Her amazing memory collects data and works like a GPS.

Maybe it's not so bad that these two are with me.

Finally we reach the exit.

Crouched down, we run for the capsule. The South Lawn is eerily empty.

"Where is everybody?" I ask, irritated but relieved that no one is guarding the capsule.

"Maybe we're no longer important," Elroy answers.

Inside the capsule, I check the battery.

"The battery is at thirty percent. That won't get us home," I say. There is only one way to get home now. "Kim, push the rescue button."

Headquarters has to pull us back to our time.

And we wait.

The last thing I hear in 2036 is the scratching sweep of the rescue ray on our capsule.

My first action after our government unsealed the 11th-hour period records based on our research, is to grab one of the tapes from the Futura-One-Library.

Sitting in my grandfather's apartment, I push in the old tape.

"Grandpa, I have something for your birthday. It's from 2036. The speech of the UN Secretary right after they saved the moon from colliding with the McKinney Asteroid."

My Grandfather nods.

The deep voice of UN Secretary Groban Nequasti sounds excited.

"Dear Global Citizens, today we celebrate a major victory. This is a wonderful day for all of us. It will change the course of humanity. I just got confirmation that we saved our moon. Together!

"We survived, not because we were the quickest, or the strongest. No! We survived because we stuck together, embraced our diversity and worked over all divisions for the good of this planet. We thank General Arthur Shoppenhauer McKinney for his tremendous positive impact to settle the issue between the United States and China.

"Over the last centuries, we mastered the art of killing. Let's now work on mastering the art of living together, with all our differences ..."

With a sigh my grandfather interrupts, "Our whole society today is built on that speech."

A warm tingle runs over me and I squeeze my grandfather's hand.

The Clearing

Mary O'Brien Glatz

It was steep going above tree line. The trail ended on a flat rock summit the size of a football field that sat higher than the cloud cover. The hike was difficult, bouldering through the keyhole then scrambling up the avalanche shoot, but it was invigorating. It was just what Muriel needed and she could handle it. Even though there was no snow reported yet in the high country, she knew the unpredictability of weather at this altitude and had started walking from the hotel long before dawn. But it was already midday when she reached the top.

Gazing out above the cumuli, she felt a tingle on her scalp and brushed a hand through her hair. Tiny sparks sputtered into the air. Static electricity was building. Black thunderheads rolled in fast from the west. Within minutes, hail was pummeling her and the handful of other hikers who had braved the peak. Lightning snapped and cracked, sizzling down all around them. The others, mostly foreign tourists, screamed and scurried.

Muriel called out, "Follow me. Crouch down. Stay low. Don't touch the ground. We can get down safely if we stick close together. Hurry!"

She put her hand out for them to form a human chain—strangers helping each other across the icy, narrow rock ledge and down the avalanche shoot, lest anyone slip. Once past that, they all followed her lead and squatted like leaping frogs down the steep trail until they were safe below treeline. They thanked her profusely and parted ways. The storm passed over the Rockies and blew out onto the plains.

Muriel picked up her pace as she headed down the mountain. The brisk pace expanded her lungs and brought a rosy glow to her cheeks. Scaling fourteeners over the years had made her an old hand at dealing with challenging conditions and rugged terrain. Reaching the top was her reward and she never feared doing it alone, despite the hazards. Her legs surged beneath her as she reflected on what had brought her here. It had been a while since she'd felt this good.

The election of a madman into the seat of power had sent her over the edge. She hadn't seen it coming. No one had. Now she didn't trust her her own instincts. The weight of her failure had almost crushed her. She had lost her composure, her voice, her health, several pounds, and a bit of her sanity this past year. By December, the strong, confident woman she knew herself to be had regressed into a newborn state of infantile vulnerability. Everything she thought she was, she was not, and everything she thought was right had turned out to be wrong. She was tired and disgusted with it all, almost ready to give up.

Battered with bad news, she had started drinking a bottle of cabernet to numb herself into a fitful sleep each night. This had been her undoing. A false alarm heart attack had landed her in the emergency room, where she had been told that it was a closing of the esophagus from too much red wine, acid reflux, and probably the prolonged stress of an ugly campaign.

Upon her release from the hospital, she had booked the first flight she could find to get out of town, get some exercise, soak up some blue sky and sun. When she had arrived at her favorite lodge nestled high in the foothills, she acknowledged that she was ready to let it all go instead of always carrying so many and lifting more than her share of the load. As her eyelids had fluttered almost shut and her mind had drifted off to an early sleep, a golden eagle had swooped over the hill into her line of sight.

Muriel snapped out of her reverie and back into the present when her hike came to an end back at the lodge. A tourist brochure in the lobby caught her eye. The big print claimed that a local shaman could clear out bad energy and connect to universal consciousness. Hah! So new age, or was it indigenously old age? Muriel wasn't sure. She had no idea what a clearing was, but why not? Rational thought, historical facts, reasonable opinions, documented truths held no sway anymore. So why not try something new, go galactic soul surfing? She called the number and made an appointment for later in the evening.

The shaman came to Muriel's room at the appointed time carrying what looked like audio equipment. She was young, demure, and beautiful. Her long dark hair framed her penetrating green eyes and graceful, angular features.

Muriel took stock of her own wrinkled, sun-mottled skin, her scraggly white hair, her smallish pot belly and sagging arms. She chuckled and decided that she was strong and beautiful in her own way, comfortable in her own skin. Muriel was known to openly protest when she heard women, but not men, judged by their age and appearance, rather than by their competence and skill. She had come to love her wrinkles. They furrowed in the wisdom of the crone and the experiences of a lifetime. But still, the young clairvoyant standing before her now emitted an uncommon radiance and a blissful serenity that Muriel had rarely witnessed.

"I want some of that," Muriel whispered to herself under her breath.

The shaman spoke.

"Please sit across from me and make yourself comfortable, Muriel. I will be your spirit guide and take you to the other side of the veil, to a dimension beyond time and space, where spirits dwell. I will tell you what I see and hear as we travel together in galactic space. You may receive the images and scenes I describe to you any way you like. You might understand them as metaphors, as past lives, or as dreams. It's up to you. I do not create the visions. I channel ancestral, eternal, galactic energies. I only narrate what I see."

Muriel smirked. "Well, I do need to clear out all the negative energy heaped on me this past year, and would love to see if there's a pathway to a better future. Can your 'clearing' do that for me?"

"What are your intentions, Muriel? I will share them with the spirit world and ask for guidance."

Muriel thought, "*My intentions? Hah! Well, they certainly have been maligned lately. Does anyone even care anymore¿'*

But she answered, "I want to be healthy, to help others be healthy, to protect the planet, live in peace with an open heart, trust in the future, have deep relationships with others, empower others to be their best, be a role model for all, and be of service to the world. I want to make a difference."

"Then let us begin," said the shaman. "Close your eyes. I will tell you what I see, and when we're done, I'll give you a recording so you can listen again later."

She switched her CD player on, then covered her own eyes with a black cloth, plugged in and put on on thick Bose headphones that pulsed native drum beats into her ears, switched on her audio recorder to capture the session, and began to chant herself into a trance state.

A moment of silence, then the shaman called out in a guttural whisper, "We enter the sacred space of the galactic stream together through the middle world and leave an offering at the sacred tree. We come here for Muriel, seeking wisdom and guidance. I offer Muriel's intentions to my galactic team of crystal beings, sacred sentinels, and power animals to guide us. I call on my healing masters and psychic surgeons to remove any barriers, dispel interfering energies, and open the stream to Muriel's energy. I call on the Akashic Record Keeper to lift the veil so that we may see. May I have permission to bring Muriel into the galactic stream?"

"Muriel, say your name three times," the shaman whispered.

Muriel whispered, "Muriel, Muriel, Muriel."

"They say, 'Yes.'" The shaman emitted a low hum. "We may continue through the gateway to the middle world, then into the stream. I see a deer who will be your gentle guide."

Muriel could almost see it in her mind. A deer with huge antlers waited silently at a gate that opened into a forest. Its eyes were wide and soft as it followed them through a wooded arbor into a stream of swirling lights, colors, and translucent shapes. They moved through the ether. She felt like she was floating, until a sudden startle jolted her head back.

The shaman cried out, "Muriel, there are energies all around us that are not yours. They are not friendly to you. They are reaching out, trying to grab you, hold on to you, inhabit you like hungry ghosts, stop you from moving forward."

Muriel felt like she was choking, her throat was closing.

The shaman yelled, "I call upon my galactic healers to clear out these foreign entities so that Muriel may pass through to her own energy, unrestrained by these others!"

Poof! A forceful, audible exhalation blew out from the shaman's mouth. The air around them cleared. Muriel swallowed. Her throat relaxed.

The shaman called out again, "Oh no, something here is very powerful, and hostile toward you. It's trying to hold you down. I feel like I'm suffocating with you, Muriel, and my heart hurts. Some entity wants to prevent you from being seen and heard, and doesn't want me to bring you further."

"I see a circle of young girls and old women, all suffering and in pain. They are crying and reaching out their arms to you as their protector. But malicious entities don't want you here. Now it looks like they're trying to cut you up and shove you into a wide mouthed red porcelain vase. The vase looks Egyptian. There are some kind of hieroglyphics or symbols on it. You keep climbing out to get away, but they keep pushing you down again and again."

"You have all this energy and wisdom that you want to share, and you have taken care of so many, but they don't want you to get out of this vase. It's as if they're cutting you up and murdering you over and over again."

"There appears to be some glitch in the system that keeps rebooting and recycling back to old events, old stories. But these are not your energies. They are eons old, ancient."

Muriel caught her breath and gasped for air with a sharp inhale.

Something wet was sliding down Muriel's cheeks. No sobbing, just a silent waterfall of tears sliding down her cheeks. She breathed in and out, trying to expand her chest from the crushing weight she felt, then snorted once and wiped her face.

"Again, I call upon my celestial guardians, psychic surgeons, and sacred sentinels to rid this space of these negative forces and pull Muriel through to her own energy stream," the shaman intoned louder, now in a different, more primitive chant.

Woosh! A vigorous gust of air forced its way across Muriel's face. She felt a lifting of the intense pressure in her chest, a release of the sharp pain in her temple, a loosening of her muscles. She breathed deep into her diaphragm and exhaled for an extra moment.

The shaman chanted for a few moments, then spoke again, "Muriel, your space has cleared. Now we can see your energies, your power animals, and your spirit guides, unclouded by those others. A soaring golden eagle has appeared to give you long vision so you can see the bigger picture."

"A phoenix has risen from ashes. Do you see all this, Muriel? These are your sacred power animals and spirit guides. Your space has opened up so that you can remember who you have always been. You are a Phoenix rising out of ashes. Oh, wait Muriel, there is more. Look! Dolphins are skimming across a shimmering aquamarine ocean and its white-capped waves. They come to remind you to laugh, to have fun, to lighten up your life with pleasure, in the good company of friends and loved ones."

Muriel expanded inwardly as her lips turned upward in a peaceful smile.

The shaman intoned, "Akashic Record Keeper, I call on you to update Muriel's soul energy and vibrational frequencies. But first I will seal her galactic space for the future." She leaned forward to brush a golden eagle feather lightly across Muriel's forehead, then touched each of her shoulders and swept it down the center of her body.

Muriel opened her eyes to wake from her trance.

The shaman was still in the chair opposite, eyes covered, headphones on. She blew out another forceful current of air toward Muriel and said, "Your celestial space has been cleared and sealed. You should rest now, Muriel. I'll email you the recording of our session."

The shaman removed her eye covering, packed up her equipment and left.

Muriel felt lighter, healthy, refreshed, happy.

The next morning, her flight left early for the dark gray skies of Washington, DC. She reached her apartment in a relaxed state, and fell into a deep sleep as soon as her head hit the pillow. The sun rose too soon as the phone rang to interrupt her vivid dreams. In a fog, she reached for it and answered, "Yes?"

It was her former press secretary.

"Muriel, you won, you won! The recount is done. All the votes are in. You won, Muriel. You are the President!"

"What? What are you talking about?" *I must be still dreaming*, she thought.

"Muriel, the recount is complete. The Commission found five percent of his votes to be fraudulent, enough to change the Electoral College, and it verified the Russian connection. And the vote was overwhelmingly *Yes* to invoke Article 25. The madman is out. The Vice President has resigned in disgrace. Thank God! Get up. Get dressed. Get down to the Capitol Building right now, Madame President!"

Muriel hung up, rose from the bed with ease, started to hum. She dressed at a languid pace, slipping on a dark navy blue suit, a crisp white shirt and delicate floral neck scarf with a flash of red. She smiled to herself as she said aloud, "Hmm, maybe we should add shamanic clearings to the services covered under the new and improved Universal Health Care Act, now that the eagle has landed."

Peer

Tanasha Martin

"No! No! No!" Giddy chastises himself in a subdued voice.

Heat burns behind his eyeballs. He blinks.

Sometimes he wishes his parents had fixed him in his mom's belly the way that other families do now. He smacks the center of his forehead, careful not to make a mark like last time. He shakes his head with enough vigor to draw attention. The sun glares in the cloudless sky. Heat climbs his neck. The notice of others at the park is fleeting, the same as when he was in the 'regular school.' Because he isn't regular. He fights the urge to hide behind his camera until the eyes go away.

Dad's voice rings in his head, "Men who shave shouldn't hide behind hands or cameras." So, he no longer shaves. He misses his dad. His features were like his: wavy brown hair, brown eyes, and dimples. Except his face is rounder. Different.

Giddy shakes the camera like he's seen people shake ink cartridges. Hope springs in his chest that it will work. The battery shaped light continues to flash red on the display. Mr. Jameson tells him each time he takes media class at the Hanes Center, "Jiggling it won't work, buddy. Number one rule of taking pictures: for the camera to work, the battery needs juice."

Giddy mumbles, "The battery needs juice." The exposed feeling grows. He sets the camera down beside him on the bench and rummages through his backpack for the cord. He travels the farthest from home to this park. Although all parks are outfitted with power towers, only a few have multiple style outlets which accommodate his cord. His eyes dart across the lightly inhabited, well-maintained park for one.

The camera, a gift from his parents, is an old model—manufactured 22 years ago. It's three years older than him. He'd asked his mom for a better one, since everything new is made to be better, but she told him that you should value what you have. Her face and voice are more elusive than his dad's. It's been a longer time since she was reduced to ashes and buried with a seed in the CemeTree. He'd watered her soft needled pine every day for a year until Dad told him that God would water her from now on.

Giddy's camera helps him capture his favorite stories - the family kind. He values them before hero stories. He refuses to miss this one. Today's story is nice. The dad with long arms and bushy eyebrows just joined the blonde lady with the swirly short hair and a baby on a blanket. They were near the swings with a basket between them. His mouth waters and he groans aloud. *There were probably cookies in there.* Giddy wants to capture them, with movement and feeling, like television. It wouldn't do to continue to record while walking. The last time he had, wood chips slid beneath his feet like sand. He'd tromped on a boy's teeny fingers. The boy shrieked and the mom yelled things so mean, Giddy bruised his forehead with the palm of his hand and got on the wrong bus home in his retreat. There would be fewer people like him soon. They make babies regular now, so little fingers will be safe.

The tower beside a red maple was free of other people and their dangling cords. Giddy shoves the plug into the only matching outlet and snatches the viewfinder to eye level. The battery icon ceases to blink and a lightning bolt marks its center. His shoulders relax and his cheeks push against the display as he settles on them, the Picnic family. They rise with the baby in Mrs. Picnic's arms and head toward the playscape, so he can still say "the End" for this story when he views it later. The muscles in his slim fingers loosen their grip as a young, thin businessman in a blue suit steps into the frame.

"How rude!" Giddy joggles the camera and hopes to jar the intrusive Suit from his story. "Move! Move! MOVE!"

Giddy slants his entire body sideways and takes his camera with him. The Suit throws away a brown paper bag and misses. He bends to retrieve it at the trash can covered with pebbles and cement, a few feet behind the couple's blanket. What he lifts is not a paper bag from the grass. Giddy zooms and spies the object of the Suit's interest: Mrs. Picnic's purse.

Giddy straightens his posture and lowers the camera. The Suit shoos a fly with one hand and peers into the purse, tilting it at slightly. Giddy stands, his camera dangling from the tips of his fingers. Coronation Park is equipped with floating black Safetycraft with recorders extending from them like wings. The crafts had eliminated the demand for actual Shields to walk the parks or neighborhoods. He missed Shields. They were smiles and pats on the back. But Safetycraft had already traveled overhead. The Suit might get caught later, but what if Mrs. Picnic needed something from her purse? What if it was for Baby Picnic? Giddy steps back and forth on the tips of his sneakers. *Somebody has to do something!*

Citizen Courage and Champion, his favorite superheros, would know what to do. Dad's voice chimes, "For Pete's Sake, Giddy, are we colored in marker? Cartoons aren't real."

Funny, the television shows that aren't cartoons aren't real either. Giddy strains to imagine himself as Citizen Courage. He is strong, brave and smart. Only people who are or made whole can be those. Maybe he could be Champion, just a little bit. He warns people and tells Citizen Courage things to help him. *I could do that.*

Giddy shuffles his feet and works up his own courage. The thud of his chest pounds a rhythm. It moves him forward. "Hey! That does not—not yours!"

The Suit finds Giddy's glare and furrows his brow. His eyes go wide. He drops the purse into the trash and takes off at a brisk walk. Giddy follows. He fumbles in his chase, leaves his backpack behind, and clutches only his camera. The cord snakes on the ground behind him. He crosses the lush grass. *Champion would catch the Suit even if he were on wood chips.*

Giddy draws nearer to the Suit. A sensation washes over him. *What do you call it where there's a word you want to say, but can't think of it right now?* Words are like that. Mr. Jameson calls them "edgers". Words or names in your brain you can't grab fast enough to use — like they'd fall off the edge of your thoughts if you get too close. The Suit feels like an edger, the closer he gets, the more familiar he seems.

The Suit slows to a walk at the outskirts of the park and crosses the street. Giddy crosses several yards behind him, landing on the curb as the traffic display terminal displays people that walk. He comes to a stop. Big streets don't scare him anymore, but this is different. There isn't enough time to prepare. Why had he run this far? What should he do? The Suit didn't actually take her purse. Why is he still chasing him? Why is the Suit still walking so fast?

The park looks huge from this side of the street, but not as enormous as the building the Suit stops in front of. Giddy cranes his neck to find the top. It's the kind that touches the clouds or scratches the sun. *No, that's not right.* It's silver with shiny windows. By the time he reaches the revolving door, the Suit is already inside. The doorman wears a silver hat and matching jacket with big black buttons. He pushes against Giddy's chest to prevent his entry.

Button's heavy accent, like the marshmallow cereal cartoon, was firm. "Sorry, lad. You're notta go 'nside. Ya don't work here."

Giddy's chest heaves. "But, Mrs. Picnic needs...;" He swallows. "Mr. Suit took...No he didn't take..He had it.... He..."

His knees waver like seaweed.

What he thought was his reflection, wears a suit. A blue one.

He also wears his face. Shaven.

Regular.

Not so scary now. What regular should look like.

The breeze is sharp, a cheese grater on Giddy's newly exposed cheeks, chin and upper lip. He owns no suit, but wears a tie, one with bunnies hopping one over another. His lips curve around minty clean teeth, and the skin on his face objects to the taut stretch. He touches the hair above his ears. It no longer curls there. He's cut it.

Giddy negotiates the street, armed with forethought, among the horde of bodies that proceed to their various destinations. He matches the flow of the people heading in the direction of the shiny building. His movements jut and lumber instead of stride like the Suit. Mr. Jameson once told him, "There are times where you may want to blend in with everyone else, but most of the time it is easier to be yourself." He was wrong. It was a lot harder to be you when the other you is regular. When the other you is better. Fixed.

He knows why his parents made this choice. They'd told him. He'd asked numerous times and was never disappointed. He didn't quite understand it all, but he was often corrected when referring to the child created from his corrected stem cells as his brother. His mother always ended the story with, "We let someone buy a copy of you because we wanted to be able to take care of you, just as you are. You were perfect for us."

But he isn't. The world sees broken. Not smart. Not a hero.

Giddy gives his reflection on the building one more check, struggles into the backpack and approaches the revolving door. *If I keep my eyes down, they won't see me.*

"I'm afraid I'm goin' t'have t'stop ya right there, pallie." Buttons holds his hand out an inch from Giddy's chest.

"I want to talk—talk to the Suit. He will talk to me today, I think." Giddy surveys the door handle beside the revolving one.

Buttons shifts to block the entrance. "Oh no ya don't. You're gointa haveta go. Mr. Williams made it clear. E'dunna wantta talk to ya."

"I just—He'll talk to me. He'll know who I am. The face hair is gone. I—I wore a tie. He'll talk to me now." Giddy moves to the revolving door and is met with the shiny, black buttons.

"Ya need t'leave or I'll be forced ta call the Shields. That's trouble you dunna want t'get inta, son." He tilts his fingers toward Giddy, commanding him to move back.

Giddy doesn't want to get IN TROUBLE. He's only been IN TROUBLE a handful of times and it isn't something he'd care to repeat. He takes a few steps back. Arms and legs stream around him in a rush, like a school of fish around a rock. He knows he should shake his feet free, but they feel immersed in silt.

Buttons speaks to him a few times before tapping the call button on his earpiece. Giddy saves his words for the Suit—Mr. Williams—Will.

The Shields are sharks on either side of him. They scatter the fish and circle him with their razored teeth. They are hulking and muscled and not at all like the ones who walked the park. The words they use are large and fuzzy and make Giddy's body sweat and quiver until his feet can mobilize.

Words like *stalking*, *harassment*, and *arrested* have no meaning for Giddy other than IN TROUBLE. He shuts the world out with his eyes and covers his face with his hands. *My ears need two hands too.* A familiar voice fades into the clutter—similar to his own. He slides moist hands down from stinging eyes and peers out through slits at Will.

Will emerges from the revolving door. This time, he dons a black suit with thin grey stripes. *It would look awesome with a cape.* Giddy swipes his face with the backs of his hands.

Will approaches with caution, eyes locked on Giddy. "What is going on here?"

Giddy's arms dangle. He straightens his back and tries to maintain eye contact without diverting. "I wanted to—to-."

A Shield with the spiky red hair steps between them. "We were dispatched to handle a nuisance disturbance, sir. Your, um, Contributor was attempting to get into the building."

Giddy jumps to the side, trips over his own feet and causes the Shield to grasp his right wrist with too tight a grip. It shifts as if it were a floating rope knotted to an anchor. At least he could see Will now. "I didn't DISTURB Will, I just—I just was walking. Buttons got me IN TROUBLE! I just wanted to talk—talk to you. I'm Giddy..." He turns to the Shield and jerks loose. "We're like—brothers, right?"

Will's gaze shifts to the men. The wind dries Giddy's exposed teeth and the streaks of salt on his skin pulls on his cheeks. Will is right here. *My normal story.* The seconds weigh like hours. Giddy tilts his head, watching Will's expression. *This must be what my face looks like when I pick between the marshmallow creme cookies or the raspberry muffins at the market. Sometimes it is hard to know what you will want tomorrow.*

Will's eyes land on Giddy with purpose. A rock forms in Giddy's stomach the size of this morning's bagel. Will's lids slide closed. "Please remove him from the premises."

Giddy removes the camera strap and unwraps the cord. "The battery needs juice." He wiggles the plug past the rust in the older tower. He plops on the splintered bench and peeks through the viewfinder. This park's play area has green tire pieces. No wood chips. It's the only thing Giddy likes about it. The grass is longer, there are fewer Safetycrafts, and the stories are less happy here.

He swings his feet back and forth, and kicks the curled, brown leaves. The viewfinder sweeps the park until it lands on a small brown boy with a tiny puppy. The boy climbs stairs of the playscape where the puppy can't follow. His ears flop with every jump as he waits at the bottom of the slide. The puppy licks his face when he lands until the boy erupts with laughter.

Giddy hits the zoom button as the boy and the puppy move further back into the play area. He stands and takes a few steps closer. The cord, taut and restrictive, tugs him back. It snaps its tether. His fingers are light. The dayls brightness sears through him. His breath catches and his mental faculties freeze.

His camera is gone.

A man in a loose green hoodie jogs from the path in front of the bench and shoves Giddy's camera into his kangaroo pocket. A quick search of the wind and overcast skies. No Safetycraft. No one will bring his camera back. "Citizens of courage and champions care" won't be proclaimed because cartoons aren't real. Acid churns Giddy's stomach. This morning's grapefruit burns his throat.

Giddy sprints after him. Sweat coats his forehead and palms. *It's mine!* He pumps his legs to match the Hood's and prays he doesn't trip.

The Hood dashes between the trees. They stand like lifeless fingers, unwilling to bend or bind. He squeezes between people and dodges a few teens on hoverskates. Giddy attempts similar maneuvers, only to elicit shrieks and curses along the way. He stumbles to the street, where the Hood walks and joins the mass that shifts and splits at the corner.

The people pictured on the traffic display video patiently wait. Those people who chew gum, check their watches, or dial their phones. *I'm not one of them. They don't need cameras!*

Giddy darts into the crosswalk and is almost to the halfway mark when screams and horns blend. They drown out all thought. When his mind unscrambles, the bone in his leg is sharp and red and SHOULDN'T BE STICKING OUT OF HIS SKIN LIKE THAT.

Faces crowd around him. Too much. Noise, eyes, and sun. The inside of his elbow and arm stretch across his cheeks. He never understands why people want others to see them. It's hard enough to see yourself, and you live with yourself everyday.

He hears a whimper. Loud — inside his own throat. A gentle tug pulls at his elbow repeatedly, but he steels it in place.

Stay here until it all goes away.

A modified version of his voice hovers. "Giddy, it's me, um, Will." Giddy's arm relaxes.

He tries to move. Skin grips exposed bone on his leg and screams in all directions. His voice matches it until he has to take in breath to replace it. He tries to stop the tears, but they slide down the sides of his face and pool in the creases of his ears anyway.

It'll be okay now. Will is here.

"I'm so sorry, Giddy." Will sets the camera on the asphalt beside him. He takes Giddy's hands in his, and squeezes them until they feel like a ball of yarn, fingers over fingers. "I did this. I just wanted to get the recording you might have of me back. Erase it or something. I never wanted you to get hurt. I swear."

Those words hold weight. They sink into Giddy's brain and slosh around until they settle like stones. An unnamed flame lights in his chest. It rivals his leg in ways he can neither understand nor voice.

Sirens wail. They pick up where Giddy's end. "You made him take my camera." He expels in a whisper. "But w-why?"

Will's brow crinkles. "The recording—"

"No, w-why did you do THAT?" Giddy persists. "Why d'you have Mrs. Picnic's purse?"

Will looks younger than he did a moment ago. Too young to wear a suit. His eyes shift to his tie. Giddy follows his gaze. The tie is yellow with tiny black diamond clusters in swirl patterns. It reminds Giddy of — bunnies.

"It's stupid." Will's grasp tightens. "I didn't have a mom. She died before the surrogate gave birth to me. It was impulsive. The purse was open. I saw pictures of their family in there. I just wanted a glimpse—at a happy family."

The Siren Doctors make quick work of Giddy's leg and question him. He answers in so small a voice, Will is compelled to repeat his responses. They warn Giddy that they are placing a lift square at the center of his back and describe what it will do. He feels the gentle expansion and cushion meld to his body and float him to waist height of the Siren Doctors. Safetycrafts hover above the accident like vultures.

Heels click on pavement and Giddy closes his eyes. He replays the Picnics in his mind and imagines himself on the blanket, cookie in hand.

I'll never wear a suit.

The lift slows and Will bumps the edge at Giddy's feet. Will touches the Siren Doctor's shoulder. "Um, is he going to be alright? I mean, if he needs anything. You know, like blood, I'm pretty sure I'm a match."

The Siren Doctor takes a long look at Will and considers them. "Contributor or related?" He presses a sequence of buttons at the open door of the ambulance and it moves the lift pad higher. Giddy and Will's eyes lock. *Cookies or muffins* pass through Will's mirrored features.

He takes a step that places him at Giddy's side.

"We're the same."

The Last Frontier

Gregory Wright

The doctor welcomed the mother and her teenage daughter into his office and encouraged them to have a seat. Tentatively they sat down in the large upholstered chairs, the mother leaning forward slightly in anticipation, the daughter thin and wide eyed, sitting in the chair next to her. The large arms seemed to envelope her and she leaned back into it as if to hide in the fabric.

"Thank you for coming in Mrs. Twain. I know this is last minute, but I have some news."

Her daughter crossed her arms over her chest, as if to protect herself from an assault. The mother leaned a little further forward, hands now clasped in her lap.

"All of the tests are in and my initial diagnosis has been confirmed, I'm afraid that what I feared," he hesitated before continuing, "is what Aloette has."

"Which is?" the mother asked softly. Here knuckles were white from the pressure of her fingers. As she shifted in her seat, a small tuft of white paper was visible, the remains of a kleenex that was beginning balled and pressured into a tiny white ball. The girl began to slide her feet back and forth, nervously, steadily, until the mother reached out and grabbed her right knee tightly. Without a look, the girl immediately stopped and sank a little lower into the vastness of the chair.

The doctor placed his hands on either side of the tablet in front of him and took a deep breath. Unknowingly his right hand began to roll the stylus from the tablet along the top of his desk. Beads of sweat began to form on his lip. His eyes darted, as if the words he needed to say were on the desk for them to see, so that he didn't need to say them.

"I'm afraid that your daughter is developing a severe case of …. acne."

The mother gasped. The daughter slowly shook her head saying "No … No" under her breath, tears began forming in her eyes. Her complexion was ashen, the corners of her mouth began to sag as she fought back the reflex to cry.

The mother turned pale and stared down at the floor as if looking to get some sort of reassurance. The doctor quietly waited, suspending any further explanation until the news had completely sunk in.

"I'm sorry."

"Isn't there a pill or something she can take to make it disappear?" the mother asked.

"This isn't cancer where we can make tumors shrink and disappear within 24 hours, or heart disease which we can reverse in a few days, or even MS where we can do our radium scans to make the symptoms disappear while people sleep." He paused for effect. "This is something that we have to address and it will take time and effort."

"So there is no normal cure?' she asked.

"If this was something easy like Alzheimer's which can be reversed over a weekend, I would prescribe it immediately. But it isn't. We have to attack it head on."

Taking some hope from the doctor's words, the mother stood up straight and reached over for her daughter's hand. The young girl, in a daze, raised a limp wrist.

The mother took in a deep breath, released it slowly and continued, "What do we do?"

"There is a series of treatments. It will take about 3-4 weeks. But it *is* effective."

"Why so long?' the daughter pleaded meekly, hopelessly. As if asking from another room.

"Young lady," the doctor replied, a little agitated. He stood up straight now, his earlier nervousness gone, and now an impatience settled in. "This isn't arthritis which we can eliminate in a few hours. It is going to take time." Turning to the mother, he calmly reassured her, "This is the last frontier in science. Who's to say there isn't a doctor somewhere in a little lab just on the verge of a discovery. You have to have hope."

The mother smiled weakly, her lips thin and taut. Her eyes narrow. Brow furrowed. Already she was mentally preparing herself for the long fight. Like a westward bound pioneer wife facing an oncoming sandstorm in her Conestoga wagon, she nodded her head in agreement. "Let's do it."

"Now," the doctor continued, speaking clinically so as not to elicit too much excitement, "Having your cooperation is critical; therefore, I need to let you know there is one other option."

Gaining courage from her mother's confidence, the daughter leaned forward, fully focused on the doctor's words. "It's new."

"Anything." The daughter said softly under her breath.

"There is a salve that could clear it up. It could be gone completely in a few hours. It would also prevent it from returning for up to two months. But you both need to understand. It's experimental." The doctor raised his hands, as if defending himself in case they vaulted over the desk.

The mother and daughter locked eyes and the mother answered for both of them, smiling and batting back tears of hope.

"Sign us up." she said firmly. The daughter now began to cry. Knowing that her mother wouldn't abandon her through this brave effort made her so proud.

"Excellent." The doctor said with a sigh of relief. "Now there is one drawback you should know about. There *is* an odor ...."

Talitha

Bonnie B. Bradlee

Talitha stood on the shore, her intense blue eyes scanning the horizon — the edge of forever. She didn't know what she was looking for, just that it was on the way. Something was "out there" and it was coming here, and it would change all of their lives, but hers most of all. Behind her, tucked safely in the jungle, the village sat unaware. The island had always been home to her family, her generation and many before her.

From the top of the coconut tree Joshua shouted, "Talitha! I see something! It's at the edge of forever, but I think it's coming this way!"

"Joshua, what are you doing up there? Remember what Gran told you about climbing trees. Do you want another week without Miguelito? Get down from there before someone sees you." Talitha hollered at her little brother.

Will that boy ever learn? Even as she thought it, she remembered herself at the age of ten, just seven years ago, knowing full well she too would have been up that tree. She smiled as he slid down, scurried to her and wrapped an arm around her lower back. She realized he was growing fast. Tall for his years, he would soon take his place among the elders of their village.

"Come on, Joshua, let's go home. Your eyes were playing tricks on you. Look, there's nothing out there."

"But Talitha, I know I saw something. It was just coming over the edge of forever. There's something else out there, I just know it. Remember when Gran talked about the thing, oh what did she call it? The perhaps? No, I remember, 'The Great Perhaps.'"

Talitha did remember, but was surprised that her brother did. That had been at least five years ago. Half his lifetime. She had been 12, on the cusp of womanhood. They sat around the village firepit listening to Gran's stories of "back then," a time that no one else remembered.

Gran was the village Grand Elder, inheriting the position when Gramps died. *Wow, seven years already. I was Joshua's age when Gramps died.* She thought about how Gran told stories from those olden days, but never talked of what happened to the others. She talked of the greatness of the village, how big it had been, how powerful they were on the island, even how the others came and gave them honor. But she never spoke of what happened, why the honor was lost. Now the village was small, weak, and no one ever came. It was as if their village no longer existed to the rest of the island. Talitha occasionally wondered about what happened. But between becoming a woman of the village and caring for her little brother, she didn't think about it for long.

Now, the siblings stood side by side, arms around each other, his around her waist, hers across his shoulders, looking out to sea, each silently wondering about the mysterious "Great Perhaps."

Slowly, Talitha turned her brother around, saying, "Come on Joshua, let's get back to the village. I have to help Mom and Gran prepare the meal for tonight. You do want to eat, don't you?"

The smile on his face was answer enough as they walked toward the village, entering the trees on the path that led to the village about a kilometer from the shore. The always pensive Talitha wondered if it was a family trait, or if she was rubbing off on her brother as he remained uncharacteristically quiet and thoughtful all the way to the edge of the village.

The path widened as they approached home. Suddenly Joshua broke free and ran to their hut where his dog had been tied up for the day. It was his punishment for climbing trees, not having Miguelito as a companion as he adventured through the jungle. Too bad the dog suffered as much as the boy for the tree climbing infractions. Miguelito was a feisty, medium sized dog with short legs and one floppy ear who jumped for joy when he saw his boy. He didn't just jump, but jumped and jumped and jumped and jumped. He was a mighty leaping dog, needing to be off running in the jungle with his boy. He had too much energy to be tied up at the hut all day.

Joshua ran to the dog who leaped into his arms, wiggling, squiggling, and washing his face with kisses. "Oh, Miguelito," the boy crooned, "I know. I'm sorry. I won't get caught climbing trees anymore. I promise."

Just inside the hut, Gran smiled. *Won't get **caught** anymore, not, won't DO it anymore.* She sighed a Gran-sized sigh. *Boys will be boys.* She caught sight of Talitha, lithe body floating along the sandy path, her long blonde hair fluttering in the breeze. A slight smile caressed her lips. *And young women will be young women as well. It's nearly time.*

Grandmother and granddaughter hugged as Talitha entered the hut, then exchanged knowing grins as Joshua called from outside, "Gran, may I please untie Miguelito? He shouldn't be punished because I was bad. He needs to run. And I'll be good. I promise."

"Okay, Joshua. See that you are good. Remember, I have eyes all over this village. And they see into the tops of trees, too." With a yelp from the boy and a bark from the dog, they were off, leaving Gran and Talitha smiling and shaking their heads as they walked through the hut and out back to the food prep area.

Momma stood stirring a pot as it simmered over an open fire. It was as if the three women were from the same bloodline, even though Momma had married into it. All were tall and thin with sharp blue eyes, and long blonde hair, though Gran's was now generously streaked with gray, and Momma's was just beginning to turn. As Talitha looked at the faces of her mother and grandmother, it was as if she looked into an aging mirror. She liked what she saw, proud to be the daughter of such greatness. Gran handed her the grinding stone and a small bucket of dried coconut. She took them to the table and began grinding flour for the biscuits that would sop up the juice of their fish stew.

As Gran prepared the chopped fruit and greens, she studied the mother and daughter who worked in front of her. "I need to tell you something," Gran started, "And I'm not sure how you're going to take it, either of you."

Mother and daughter stopped their work, turning their attention to the matriarch of the family. "What is it, Gran?" Momma asked, "Just say it."

"Look at your daughter. She's a beautiful young woman. She's intelligent, she's talented, she deserves more than she can get here on this island."

Momma and Talitha looked at each other, then at Gran. These were confusing words for them, all they had was the island. Gran continued, "There is something beyond this island, a way out, a way off."

Suddenly, Poppa appeared on the back trail with a small buck over his shoulders. The women greeted him with grins and hugs, then turned their attention to the provision that just came in. The man in their lives, father, husband, son, was home safely from a successful hunting trip. The buck meant so much more than simple relief from the ever present fish stew. There would be new shoes, or shirts, and items available to sell or barter for other household necessities. Even Miguelito would get a new bone or two. Everybody was happy when Poppa brought home a buck. However, they knew they would have to return to the conversation that was left hanging.

"Poppa, you are such a good provider," cooed Momma, "but there's no time to dress that now. Go clean up. Dinner is nearly ready. You can deal with the buck after we've eaten."

"Yes dear," responded Poppa, "but it would be more enjoyable to dress this buck on an empty stomach, in anticipation of filling my stomach with some of its meat. I guess I'll have to deal with one more meal of fish stew." His nose wrinkled slightly as he said that, and there was a wink at Talitha and a sly grin on his leathery, weather worn face. With a quick kiss on his wife's cheek, he strode off toward the freshwater creek that flowed down from the high hill behind their hut.

Soon Miguelito came bounding back, Joshua trailing behind, running as fast as his legs would carry him. The family gathered for dinner, father and son sitting at the table waiting while the women put the finishing touches on the meal and presented it for approval. They grinned, knowing that even though it was fish again, it would be delicious, flavored with the love of the women who prepared it. And they knew that tomorrow they would NOT be eating fish!

The family sat around the rectangular table made of lashed together bamboo, enjoying each other, discussing their adventures of the day. Poppa enthralled them with a story of tracking and bringing down the buck, Momma expounded on the beauty she observed while harvesting the fruit that made up their salad. Gran began a tale from when the village was great. Suddenly Joshua interrupted, "Gran, tell us about the Great Perhaps. I'm old enough now. I'm sure of it. Where is it? Is it over the edge of forever? I saw something coming from there when I was at the top of the coconut tree..." He stopped, hand shooting up to cover his mouth, too late. The words were already out. Sadly, he looked down at Miguelito and said, "Sorry, boy."

Talitha cast her eyes down, shaking her head slightly, wishing her brother would learn to keep his mouth shut. Neither of the youngest generation saw the looks of shock, even horror on the faces of the elders for broaching the forbidden subject.

"Boy! What are you talking about? What did you see? Where was it? When?" demanded Gran.

"I'm sorry. I didn't mean to climb the tree. It just happened."

"What tree? Where were you? How long ago?" Gran asked again, clearly more anxious about the details than the fact that he had climbed again.

"At the shore. Talitha was looking out to sea. She looked so sad because she couldn't see anything. So I climbed the tree to see if I could see farther.

And I could. I saw a speck at the edge of forever. She didn't believe me, but I know I saw it. It came right up over the edge. Is that where the Great Perhaps is at, Gran? I remember when you said that, that people were seeking the Great Perhaps."

Then he saw the look of shock and disbelief on Gran's face. "They're coming," she whispered, "It's happening again."

As they sat, silent, waiting for Gran to continue, they heard footsteps coming up the path. The children looked to their parents, fear evident on their faces. The parents looked to Gran, not as fearful as the children, but definitely concerned.

Gran hung her head. "Don't worry, they won't hurt us, as long as they get what they want." Looking at Talitha, the barest hint of a smile on her face, she continued, "And they will. They will get what they want."

Talitha felt oddly comforted that Gran's sadness was tinged with pride. She wasn't sure what was about to happen, but she realized that the rest-lessness she felt while looking out to sea was quelled by her grandmother's voice and the sound of the approaching footsteps.

They all watched, waiting for the footsteps to come around the corner of the hut. All were shocked, but none so much as Poppa, when the first person to come into view was the spitting image of Poppa himself, but older. The others looked from one to the other, not understanding. But Gran knew. And her heart swelled. The stranger who was no stranger looked at her, smiled, and said, "Hello Mother." Rushing together, they crashed in a hug that crossed the decades of their separation.

The family stood in stunned silence, watching and wondering at a mother and son reunited. They waited patiently, but with deep, deep confusion. Well, all were patient but one. Is there such a thing as a patient ten year old?

"Gran. GRAN! Who is this man? He looks like Poppa! He called you Mother! Is this your son? Does Poppa really have a brother? That means I have an uncle! Hurray!! I've always wanted an uncle. Uncle! Uncle? Uncle what? What's your name? Where have you been? Where did you come from? Have you been at the Great Perhaps?"

"Joshua! Stop."

"Is it over the edge of forever?"

"Joshua! I said STOP!!"

The tone of his father's voice made Joshua stop and sit down, though somewhat miffed, not understanding why no one else was as excited as he at the presence of this newfound relative. Poppa stared, emotions playing across his face. Shock, fear, confusion, wonder, along with some of the excitement that so affected his son.

"Mother?"

Gran lifted her head from where it lay, nestled on her long missing son's chest. She looked deep into the eyes of the son she had spent her life with and said, "Yes, Joshua. This is your uncle, your Uncle James. He's your father's older brother. He went over the edge of forever when your father was just an infant. And now he's come to take all those who want to seek the Great Perhaps back over the edge with him," and she began to cry.

The shock and confusion grew. No one had ever seen Gran cry. Joshua walked to his Gran, arms circling her waist, and said, "Don't worry, Gran. I won't leave to seek the Great Perhaps. Me and Miguelito will stay here with you. And Talitha too. Right Talitha?"

There was no answer. Joshua turned to look at Talitha as he repeated, "Right Talitha? Tell Gran you'll stay here with us."

And there was still no answer. All eyes turned to the young woman, boring into her, waiting to hear her say she would stay. It was Talitha's turn to have an array of emotions shooting through her young body as if she'd been struck by lightning during a storm. Self conscious and very confused by everything she was seeing and hearing, she turned and ran, through the hut and down the path, running to the beach where she'd been drawn that afternoon. To the place where her soul stirred, wondering what else might be out there.

She stood, looking out to the edge of forever, where the moon was just rising, sending a reflected stream of light, like a beam across the water, drawing her to that edge. The boat that had brought her uncle back to his original home gently bounced in the waves along the shore. She realized that she would be leaving in that boat. She would leave her home, everyone, and everything she had ever known. She was one who would seek the Great Perhaps. And suddenly she understood. The Great Perhaps was more than just a place over the edge of forever. It was a feeling, or rather a knowing. A knowing that there is something greater out there. Something greater than this place, something greater than these people, something greater, even, than the love she had for her family. And she needed to seek it out. She needed to go and see it for herself.

As she stood, watching the moonbeam, feeling drawn to it, looking to see if it illuminated anything over the edge, the family came, standing at the edge of the beach, not quite there, but no longer on the path either.

Uncle James moved behind her, speaking gently, "Talitha, I know what you're feeling inside, the fear and the excitement. I know because I've been there. The Great Perhaps really exists. It's like another world, so different from ours, and so much bigger. Opportunities are great there. More of us were ready to go last time, perhaps too many. The village lost so much. That's why we waited so long before coming back. But if you are ready, we will show you the rest of the world, help you to learn and to grow. Then, in the future, you can be the one to come back and introduce others to the Great Perhaps."

Gran took a step forward, "Talitha?"

She turned, the reflected moonbeam shining through her golden hair, creating a halo around her head. She smiled at them, saying with a confidence she had never felt before, "I go to seek a Great Perhaps."

Bear

S. Ellen J.

I remember the day Bear came to the shelter. The Humane Society found him abandoned in a back yard, no food or water, his fur matted and muddy. The techs shaved him, got him cleaned up, and had him checked out by a vet. He was middle aged, judging by his teeth, but overall with no health problems. When it came time to test his temperament, that's when I was called in.

Most shelters used brainchord technology to tell how an animal felt, if it was mean or nice or somewhere in the middle. Angry dogs produced harsh static from the machine, while happy hounds resulted in sweet whistles, not unlike bird song. But Bear was different. When the shelter staffed turned the wavelator on him, it produced nothing. No sound, silence. It was rare, but there were some animals that wavelators could just not score, and no one had yet figured out why. And so the task fell to me, an old-timer from before the mass adoption of brainchording, to judge him the old-fashioned way.

He wasn't friendly. He was aloof, and ignored people. Other dogs? Forget about it. It wasn't as if he was aggressive, he was just not friendly. He'd ignore dogs if they were far enough away, but if they were close or if they looked at him wrong, he'd snap at them. It scared a lot of the volunteer help, and meant he had to be walked alone. He wasn't mean by any stretch, nor was he afraid. He just seemed disinterested, staring into the distance as he endured everything.

He was labeled as a Chow Chow mix, though I wasn't convinced he wasn't pure bred. He had beautiful, golden caramel colored fur once we got him cleaned up. He was beautiful to look at once his fur started to grow back, but it was difficult to get him adopted. The staff named him Bear because that's what he looked like — a big, shaved teddy bear.

No one really made a connection with Bear. Families would ask to see him, impressed by his beautiful coloring, but would be turned off by his standoffish nature and the lack of a glowing brainchord score. He'd pay no attention to anyone, and would instead sit in the corner of the visitation room.

Then one day, an elderly gentleman came to the shelter, looking to adopt a dog. He lived out in the country along the river, and wanted something to guard the house. He said he wanted a low-energy dog, too, one that wouldn't need long walks or a lot of playtime.

"I'm no spring chicken," he said. "I can't keep up with a little dog anymore."

I and an on-staff kennel worker introduced him to a few dogs. He didn't seem all that interested in the first couple of pit mixes we brought him or in the lab. I don't know why, but something in my gut said to show him Bear.

"Bear? He'll never go for Bear," said the kennel attendant. "He can't keep up with the grooming."

"Let's just try it," I told her.

We introduced them, and Bear did what he usually did. The old man called his name, whistled, and snapped his fingers to get the dog's attention, but aside from a cursory glance and a twitch of the nose, Bear gave him no attention. Bear circled the room and laid down behind the chair where the old man sat. The old man watched him, and I watched the old man. There was a certain sparkle in his eye.

"That's a good guard dog," said the old man.

Afraid I had heard him wrong, I asked, "What did you say?"

"I said, he's got a strong, protective instinct. See him sitting there? Right where I can't see. He's watching my back." The old man let out a little chuckle.

Trying to hide a smile, I looked to the kennel attendant. She pursed her lips. This confused me. I thought she would be happy for someone to like Bear. We asked if he wanted to see any more dogs, and he said no, he quite liked this one. I was ready to sign Bear over then and there, but the kennel attendant instead stepped into the conversation.

"Why don't we have you fill out some more paperwork, and then we'll plan a visit to see your house and make sure it's dog-friendly."

The man agreed, and as he wrote his address and a good time during which we could visit, I took the kennel attendant aside.

"What's wrong?"

"I know how people in his neck of the woods treat dogs. They tie them outside all the time. Bear doesn't deserve that, not after what he's been through. He needs a family and a loving home, an indoor home."

I said, "Bear will have a fine life. He'll get fed every day, he'll have water and a dog house. He may not live in the lap of luxury, but it's still miles better than staying at the shelter all his life. Listen, Bear is the perfect kind of dog for this guy."

"Bear deserves better."

"Maybe so, but let's not reject 'good' out of searching for 'best.' Let's visit this guy's house and find out more about him, and try to keep an open mind."

We stopped by the man's house on the agreed-upon day. It was just a small thing, a quaint little cape cod cottage, painted brown, on the hillside overlooking a river. The tiny yard was fenced in chainlink. There wasn't much in the way of landscaping, but the lawn was mowed.

The old man must have been waiting for us to pull up in our van, because he opened the door to meet us before we even knocked. He invited us in, and we exchanged simple pleasantries. Nothing in his house looked dangerous to dogs. We had the typical suggestions, like keeping shoes in a closet so as not to tempt the dog to chew. The man just shrugged it off. We then asked him to show us where the dog would be sleeping, and he very kindly showed us a blanket on the floor. A few old dog toys were resting on top of it, just a chew bone, a squeaky toy, and a rubber ball, nothing fancy, nothing expensive. The man showed us the dog house he had outside. It was a home-made affair, with a slanted roof instead of the pointed ones. It looked as though he made it himself, a long time ago and for a different dog.

I told him my coworker and I had a few things to discuss, and we would be right back. She still didn't like the idea. She thought Bear was too big for the little old man, too much hair, and too stubborn. We debated back and forth for several minutes, and after I pointed out how the old man had all the necessities ready before we even arrived, she conceded that the man would be a good owner. With pursed lips, she begrudgingly consented to letting him have Bear.

As my coworker fetched the dog from the van, I had one last chat with the old man. "I should warn you, Bear isn't the most affectionate dog. He's not going to sit and cuddle with you on the couch."

"Oh, that's all right. I just need something to need me. A reason to get out of bed in the morning, that's all. I know I said I wanted a dog for protection, but the truth is, it's not the thought of getting robbed that scares me; no, I've got nothing and no one ever comes out this far who wants to cause trouble. Ever since my wife died, it was just me and my dog. Now that he's gone, I'm all alone. Just being alone is what's scary, thinking I could go to bed and never wake up, and no one would care. That's why I think I need another dog. It's something to take care of. Something that needs me to keep a-going."

Before I had a chance to respond, the kennel attendant brought Bear in, and Bear did what Bear always did; he ignored everything. The old man didn't seem upset as the honey-colored dog stared at the place with that thousand-yard stare of his. The old man didn't seem at all worried when Bear showed no interest in the bed or the toys or the food and water dishes. He took Bear outside and then came in to say goodbye to us.

My partner expressed her worry again as we left. "That bed and toys were all for show. That dog will probably never come inside again."

"Even if he doesn't, he'll be taken care of," I reassured her. "He'll have food and water and a roof over his head. It's more than some dogs get. And out of any dog, he's the best for this because he's not going to miss being indoors."

For months I was just curious and concerned about Bear's fate. Without a brainchord review for Bear, I second-guessed my own gut instinct and started doubting my own abilities. Had I made the right decision? Was my coworker actually right? When it came time for Bear's six-month check-up, I insisted on going.

The kennel worker and I went back to the old man's house. We pulled up and knocked, but there was no answer. We then went around to the side and peered over the fence. There was a small tree planted there now, with stay-ties to keep it upright, and the old dog house had been remodeled, but I didn't dwell on it for my attention soon turned to Bear. His fur was so dirty, the golden color was gone. The kennel worker pointed the wavelator at Bear, and the two of us held our breath that maybe, just maybe, it would work this time, but there was only silence from the hand-held machine.

We were in the middle of discussing whether or not we should trespass to get a closer look when a car pulled up and the old man got out of the passenger's seat. He waved and hailed us, and apologized for being late. He explained how he had to get a ride from his neighbor to go to the store for some supplies, and we helped him carry in his shopping bags. We asked about the state Bear was in. The old man explained how the dog had fought with a skunk the night before, so he ran to the store for some anti-skunk stink shampoo. He had hoped to be back to give Bear a bath before we arrived, but there just hadn't been enough time.

"Does Bear stay outside all the time?" The kennel worker asked. "Because you can avoid situations like that if you let him sleep inside."

"He doesn't want to come in," the old man explained.

He then showed us what he meant by opening the back door and calling Bear, but the dog made no move to come in. The man propped the screen door open and came back to chat with us for a little bit, but Bear did not come in.

"He likes it out there," the old man said. "It's his home."

I was satisfied that Bear was in good hands, that he wasn't being tortured. The man was happy. Bear seemed to not care. Even my coworker had to agree that, all things considered, this really was a good home for Bear. It might not have been what she imagined for him, and it might not have been the perfect success story the shelter liked to publicize, but it was good enough.

Months passed, and thoughts of Bear became fewer and farther between. There were many more animals that needed help, and Bear was something of a closed case. It came as a surprise for me when I realized his one-year visit was approaching. Again, I asked to be sent out, and invited the kennel worker to come with me.

As we pulled up to the brown house overlooking the river, a heart-warming sight awaited us. The once-brown house sported a fresh coat of yellow paint, and beds of flowers had sprung up beneath the window sills. Standing in the open doorway was the old man, and at his side was a caramel colored Chow Chow. The man waved.

"You know, he remembered you," the old man said as we approached. "He barks whenever someone comes to the house now. He didn't bark when you came."

It never ceases to amaze me how some of the best techniques in life are also some of the oldest. Brainchord technology let us humans understand what our pets were thinking on a deeper level than ever before, but in this moment, it was completely unnecessary. Dogs had been communicating with us long before the invention of wavelators, and even with their primitive means of expression, managed to make their feelings known. To this day, I truly believe it is the most effective measure of their happiness.

Bear wagged his tail.

Free

Tim Yao

Benji softly closed the front door behind him. Maybe he would make it to his room for some sleep without running into Catherine. At this hour, Mom was already at work, but Catherine worked in her studio in the back of the house.

Benji tip-toed across the polished, old, hardwood floor.

Creak!

Damn!

"Hello, Benji."

Catherine put down her sketchbook and rose from her chair in the den to intercept him.

Benji ignored her and hurried up the stairs to get to his room.

Catherine swiftly followed him and put one hand on his door, preventing him from closing it.

"I'm really wiped, Catherine," he said without looking back at her. "I just want to sleep."

"We need to talk, Benji."

Benji groaned but let go of the door and flopped down on his bed. "I've been up all night."

"This is the fourth night this week!" She moved clothes off of his desk chair so she could sit.

Benji turned his head to look at her with his bleary eyes.

93

"You're letting your life slip away," she said.

"Mom doesn't mind."

"You know that Irene has tried to talk with you about this. Your mother and I both love you and are concerned about you."

"I'm just taking a break from school, Catherine."

"You took the summer off, Benji. You told us you would start classes again this fall."

He closed his eyes.

"This constant gaming is an addiction, and I don't think Mary has been a good influence on you."

"She's *my* girlfriend. You don't get a say."

"You're not yet twenty-one, Benji..."

"What, you want me to move out early?" Benji sat up and ran his fingers through his unruly, dark hair.

Catherine sighed. "Of course not. This is your home. Irene and I are happy to have you live with us. It's just that you have some real talent with your movie making. I hate to see you let it go to waste."

Benji glanced over at his home studio, which boasted connections to AIs that were far beyond what he'd be able to afford on his own without help. He hadn't touched them in months.

"I thought you enjoyed making movies, Benji."

Benji rubbed his eyes. "I'm just taking a break from that. Don't I get a say in what I do with my life?"

Catherine squeezed his shoulder. "Of course you do. But what you're doing isn't healthy. You can't stay up all night to play games week after week."

"It's 2042, Catherine. No one has to work any more. Why can't I spend time with my friends? UBI frees us up to enjoy ourselves."

"You're a creator, Benjamin Elliot Anderson, not some wastrel."

"You dare insult my friends?!" Benji groaned and stood up. "I'm not going to get any sleep here today, am I? Audrey, fetch me an ubr." He saw Audrey's icon flash green in his retinal implant.

"I'm not trying to keep you from your nap, Benji."

"Too late!" He stomped down the stairs.

"Benji!"

He slammed the front door as he exited. The grey ubr was already pulling over in front of their home. It quietly whirred to a stop in front of him, its skin shifting to assume Benji's trademarked red and golden dragon motif upon its exterior.

His stepmother's constant haranguing about his future... it was enough to make him scream. Why did he need to amount to anything? UBI. Universal Basic Income and free housing covered all his needs. And as soon as he turned twenty-one next month, he'd be able to move out and get his own place. He even had managed to save some of his UBI, following his mother's guidance.

The overlay of Audrey, his AI, was in the ubr before he entered. Her voice, modeled on Audrey Hepburn, asked, "Where to, Benji? Your blood pressure is elevated. Maybe you'd like to go to the forest preserve?"

"Yeah, sure." Benji rubbed his face in his hands. Mom would be angry about the escalating tension between him and Catherine.

"Catherine has your best interests at heart," Mom had told him only last week. "She's your mother too."

It had taken a lot for him to hold his tongue at that. *No she's not! She's just your wife!*

After all, Mom hadn't consulted with him before proposing to Catherine, just as she hadn't consulted with him when she divorced Marion three years ago. Worse, Marion had moved to Europe and she rarely called or wrote to him these days. Benji counted to ten, breathed and forced his hands to uncurl from tight fists. Maybe things in their home would have been smoother if Catherine had an outside gig; but, as an artist, she spent a lot of time at her home studio. And, now that Benji had dropped out of school, they collided too frequently.

It's my life! I can always go back to school anytime.

Some minutes later the ubr slowed and stopped. Benji emerged, standing at the edge of the forest. Three trails began just steps away. The autumn air was slightly cold, crisp and clean. He loved this time of year. The leaves were so spectacular. He yawned and walked forward, taking the left hand trail. Behind him, the ubr silently closed up and sped off, its skin fading to a neutral grey.

Damn Catherine anyway. Why can't she just leave me alone?

A small white circle appeared at the edge of his vision, projected by his implanted lenses. He saw his mom's sigil there, a highly stylized calligraphic rendition of "Irene."

"Hi, Mom," he said.

Her voice calmed him as it always did. "Hi, Benji. Catherine told me that you were upset."

"Why no visual?"

"I'm at work, remember? I can't release a penny drone here, honey."

"Oh, yeah." Mom worked at Noweicsson, the leading robotic control corporation. Security was very strict there. With a glance, he disabled his own visual and his penny drone returned to its magnetic perch in his belt buckle.

"Benji, please don't do anything rash."

"Catherine won't stop nagging me, Mom. I wish I was twenty-one already."

"You don't mean that, Benji. She cares about what you do and what happens to you. So do I."

"I'm just playing games with my friends. It's not like I'm doing drugs."

The emoji for a small location request registered beside the light green circle representing Irene's call. Benji approved it with a focused glance at the approval icon beside it.

"I'm just taking a walk, Mom. I haven't run away from home."

"I'm glad to hear that, Benji. Please come home for dinner tonight. We can have a chat. And I'll talk with Catherine to get her to ease up. Okay?"

"Okay, Mom."

"Oh, and don't forget—you promised to take Grandpa out today."

Benji winced. "Oh, yeah. No worries, Mom." He took a step forward and promptly bumped into a tall, red-haired girl.

"Hey! Watch where you're going!"

"Uh, sorry," he muttered. "I was taking a call."

"I could tell," she said. "You're lucky you didn't go out into the street and get hit by an ubr."

He snorted. "They have safety mechanisms."

"And you just like to test them from time to time, right?" She shook her head, causing her hair to move in intriguing ways.

He noticed the art bag over her shoulder. "You're an artist?"

"I came here to draw."

"I'm, ah, taking in the fall foliage," he said, adding, "I had an argument with one of my moms."

"Still living at home, eh? Are you a student?"

"Taking a break from studies, actually. I'm not sure what I want to study next."

One delicate eyebrow rose slightly.

"Look, I'm sorry for bumping into you. But I'm glad to have met you." Benji bit his lip then held out his hand. "My name's Benji," he said.

She looked down at his outstretched hand for a moment before taking it briefly in her own cool hand.

"I'm Rachel."

"Are you in school, then?"

She turned her cool gaze at him. Benji saw in that moment her eyes were a brilliant green.

She turned away. "Look, Benji, I don't want to be rude, but I'm here to draw."

He reached for her sketchbook. "May I?"

Rachel nodded. Her sketchbook wasn't digital but made of real paper, with cardboard covers.

"Ah, so you work in physical media." He gently flipped through the pages. "Hey, you're very talented."

"Thanks."

A flashing white circle caught his attention. There was no sigil, but he knew it was a reminder from his Mom. Benji sighed. *Grandpa*.

"I'm sorry, Rachel," he said. "I've got to go." He handed her the sketchbook.

Rachel shrugged and walked on.

"Audrey, ubr to Grandpa," he muttered.

Audrey Hepburn's cool voice spoke into his ear, "I'm two minutes away."

Seven minutes later, his ubr let him out at the faux brownstone apartment building. His grandfather sat outside the building in his chair, its wheels unfolded into their robotic stepping legs to help him navigate the steps.

"Hi, Grandpa," Benji said. "Looks like you're ready for our outing."

"You're late, boy."

George Anderson had always been a larger than life figure in Benji's life. Even with his withered legs, his outsized personality and booming voice had made a big impression on Benji in his childhood. Now, suddenly, Benji was aware of his grandfather's advancing years. The old man looked thin, frail.

"I'm sorry, Grandpa," Benji said.

George grimaced. "Let me guess—another domestic quarrel? Did you at least win this time?" He chuckled.

Benji shook his head. "I don't think there are ever any winners in those fights, Grandpa."

"You're sounding wiser each time I see you, kid." George coughed. "So, where are you taking me?"

"Do you need anything downtown? Or at the mall?"

"Why don't we go to the forest preserve? It looks like the trees should be in full fall foliage." Benji called an ubr and, before long, he was back at the forest preserve, this time with his grandfather.

George's chair's legs folded themselves back into wheels. He looked up at Benji. "You want to take Trail #1? Trail #2 or Trail #3?"

"How about Trail #2, Grandpa?" *Trail #2 leads to the lake. Maybe Rachel went that way.*

"Trail #2 it is."

The two of them made their way down the trail. The air was sweet here and Benji listened to the birdsong around them.

"So how are things between you and your girl? Mary, isn't it?"

Benji looked away. "It's been Mary for two years, Grandpa."

"Why so it has, so it has. Seems like the blink of an eye, though. Everything fine?"

"Yeah." Benji rubbed his arm, trying to keep his face blank as he remembered how Mary yelled at him only two days ago. "Say, how about with you and Anne? She still treating you right?" He grinned.

George made a rude gesture. "I tolerate robots only when I'm forced to. Now, if you could actually make her look like Anne Tyler and not just give her Anne's voice, that would be different."

"I could project Anne's face on her, Grandpa."

"On that little bowling ball of a head?" George sighed. "I'm too old for this anyway."

"You feeling okay?"

George looked up at Benji with a crooked smile. "I'm out here with you, aren't I?" His cackle degenerated into a coughing fit.

"Maybe it would be good to find a park bench to sit on."

George nodded. Ahead of them was a short wooden bench, occupied on one end by a tall, red-haired girl, intently working on something in her sketchbook.

"How about here?"

George drove his chair over to the side away from Rachel. Benji sat down heavily beside her.

Rachel turned an annoyed glance his way.

"Benji, what's gotten into you? Apologize to the young lady."

"Sorry," Benji said, but he couldn't help smiling.

George harrumphed. "Miss," he said. "I apologize on behalf of my rude grandson."

"That's not necessary, sir," Rachel said. "But thanks anyway."

"I hope he didn't ruin your painting."

Rachel shook her head. "No, sir. My brush was lifted when he sat down."

"May I see your painting?" George asked, moving his chair in front of Benji.

"Sure." Rachel turned her sketchbook to George.

Benji saw a vivid painting of the pond before them, executed with bold colors and strong strokes.

"Very nice," George said. "Do you sell your work?"

"Some of it," Rachel said. "Are you interested?"

"If it is something affordable, sure."

"Grandpa doesn't have a computer implant," Benji said. "So if you want to beam me your details, I can get them to him."

Rachel didn't even acknowledge Benji but instead reached into a pocket of her sketchbook and pulled out a paper card. She handed this to George.

"Thank you," George tucked it into his pocket and then turned to Benji. "I, ah, need to attend to a call of nature. I'll come back here in a few minutes, okay?"

Benji nodded, glad that he didn't have to help his grandfather. He watched his grandfather's chair recede back up the trail to the parking lot. Turning back to Rachel, he noticed a subtle marking on the paint stylus she held. Though it had the shape of a traditional paint brush, it used nano-color technology to apply color to the paper rather than paint. Through combinations of light pressure from her thumb and forefinger, Rachel could control the color, size and shape of the art she created.

"Nice multibrush," he said to Rachel. "The Xavier is an expensive model."

Rachel paused in working on her painting of the lake and turned to him. "How is it that you know about multibrushes? Are you an artist as well as a student?" Her fingers played over the sensor interfaces that controlled the brush's color, flow and dimensions.

Benji saw the tip shift from a dark blue to a muddy grey. "My stepmother is a professional artist. She has one like that."

Rachel held out her multibrush and looked at it. "This was a gift from my teacher."

"You must be an exceptional student. It would take months of savings to buy one of those."

Rachel smiled, which made her face light up and Benji's heart skip a beat. She said, "I enjoy painting, though I know that robots can create art that is so much better than this."

Benji smiled. "That's not the point of art, is it? I mean, it's just like when cameras appeared on the scene. Cameras were never able to replace all paintings and other art forms."

Rachel looked at him appraisingly. "Are you anti-robot?"

Benji snorted and grinned. "Naw. I know we owe AI and robots a lot for all they do for society. Without them, we wouldn't have basic income and the freedom to do what we want with our lives."

"Do you ever wonder what you would have done back then? I mean, we're only the second generation to experience this freedom. My grandfather and grandmother tell me stories of what their lives were like."

"My grandpa doesn't like to talk about that time." Benji made a face. "But I learned about it in school. I imagine I might have been an engineer like my mom."

"Wait, I thought you said your mother was an artist."

Benji grinned. "No, I said my stepmother Catherine was an artist. My mom is an engineer at Noweicsson."

"Your mother actually works? I mean in a job?"

"Yeah, she works with robots and AI."

Rachel frowned. "Wait. You said your stepmother, the artist, her name is Catherine?"

"Yeah?"

"What's her last name?"

"Anderson. That is, she took my mom's last name when they married two years ago. Before that she was Catherine Hsiung."

Rachel snorted, then chuckled, shaking her head. "Wow. I can't believe it. So you're that talented son my mentor mentioned."

Benji smiled and leaned back. "What a small world, eh?"

Rachel's eyes narrowed a little. "Wait. Is Catherine the one you argued with?"

Benji sighed. "She may be a good artist, but... well..." Was that a look of judgement in her eyes? Benji forced a small chuckle. "So she said I was talented?"

Rachel ran her free hand through her red hair. "Parents usually just want the best for their children."

"I'll have you know I turn twenty-one next month. Catherine thinks I'm not applying myself." He snorted. "She needs to realize that now we have a supportive society, we don't need to do anything. We can just enjoy life."

Rachel pursed her lips for a moment. "What do you do then? How do you spend your time?"

"I enjoy games," Benji said. "Movies. Spending time with friends." He gave Rachel a quick glance and then muttered. "And sex. Sex is fun."

Rachel shook her head and stood up.

Benji scrambled to his feet. "Not everyone is artistic, you know." He lightly touched her forearm. "You shouldn't judge me."

"You remember History class from school, don't you? There were many protests. The U.S. went through a very turbulent time. Oligarchs took over the government. Their policies cost a lot of people their lives."

"I know. The Second Great Depression."

"If it hadn't been for the massive, organized protests, we never would have gotten the basic income, free housing, and free education—all paid for by the massive productivity boost of robots and AI coupled with nearly limitless inexpensive energy. Poverty and homelessness wouldn't have been eliminated."

This was when Grandpa lost the use of his legs. "And now that we have these benefits, there is absolutely no reason why I should stress myself trying for a corporate or government job."

She rolled her eyes. "I wasn't talking about jobs, Benji."

"No, you were talking about art. I told you—I don't have any artistic talent. Not like that."

"It's not just about art. It's about science. There are so many pursuits for people to do with our allowance." She looked at him. "And Catherine said you were very talented."

Benji shook his head again. "I'm not an engineer. I'm not a scientist. I don't paint. And I don't have to do anything."

"Don't you feel like you're letting your life slip away?"

"You sound just like Catherine. You don't get it, Rachel. We're all free to do what we want. Freedom. It means I don't have to do something that you might regard as useful to society."

"Just a perpetual vacation your whole life."

"Isn't that what life is all about? The human part of living?" Benji bent down, picked up a small rock and winged it across the meadow at a moth. He missed. "Why do you care what I do, anyway?"

"I never said I cared," Rachel said. She brushed at her shoulder-length red hair.

"Somehow you sound disappointed."

Rachel snorted. "I don't even know you. How could you..." She rolled her eyes and then stamped off to a wooden bench further around the shore of the small pond.

Benji turned to follow her. A call circle appeared in his vision with Mary's sigil, which was an anime-styled avatar of her angry face.

He hesitated for a moment, angry again and sad. But Mary had made her choice two days ago. Cursing, he sent a focused glance at the status icon and shifted his online status to read "busy." Then he walked down to the pond and sat beside Rachel, who didn't look up from her sketchbook, where she was painting a new picture.

He watched in silence as she quickly painted the pond before them. Her strokes were bold, agitated in contrast with the placid water and quiet trees around the pond.

Mary tried three times more to reach him before her call attempts ceased.

Benji shook his head and then turned to Rachel. "Uh, you're very good," he said at last.

Rachel raised an eyebrow but didn't respond.

"Look," he said, running his fingers through his hair. "I think we got off on the wrong foot. Could we start over? Please?"

Rachel took a deep breath, then capped her brush and put it down in her case. "Okay." She held out her hand and he shook it. "Hi, I'm Rachel."

"Benji."

"I don't want to lead you on, Benji." She gave him a small smile. "You're cute, true. But I get the impression that we are at different stages of our lives."

"I didn't tell you this before," he said. "But I do some remixing work on the side."

"What media?"

"Mostly games. Some movies and short films."

Rachel reached into her bag and pulled out a thin tablet. "Show me."

"Ah, so you do have some tech!" He grinned. "Movie portfolio alpha alpha one. Offer to Rachel's tablet."

A white circle lit up on the tablet's surface with text displayed beside it.

"Text interface?" Benji chuckled.

"I'm old fashioned about some things," Rachel said. She touched a green button to the side of the circle. The tablet's surface filled with moving icons. Rachel thumbed through the listing, finally selecting a remix of the movie *Sabrina*.

"I did that for my moms," Benji said. "For their twentieth anniversary. They both enjoy old movies." His voice grew wistful, thinking of Irene and Marion before their divorce. "I replaced Julia Ormond with Audrey Hepburn in the 1995 film."

Rachel watched a scene.

"Nice work," she said at last. "It looks quite seamless."

"That's the AI at work. My mom got me access to a Hollywood-level AI."

"I'm surprised you didn't mention this earlier, Benji. Even with AI-assistance, it takes real talent to make something like this."

Benji looked down. "Well, it's been some months since I last did anything in this area." He raised his head and gave Rachel a rueful smile. "In fact, this is one of the reasons that I'm here now. Catherine thinks I'm wasting my talent by not using it."

"So why did you stop?"

Benji shook his head. "It's just a short break."

Rachel lifted her brush. "I can't imagine taking a break from my art."

"It's complicated."

Rachel stood.

Benji looked up at her, hoping she wouldn't leave.

She smiled and extended a hand to him, to help him rise.

He took her hand, stood, and didn't release it. Hand in hand, they resumed walking around the pond.

Twenty minutes later, they had made it all the way around.

"Oops," Benji said.

George sat there in his chair, arms folded but a small smile on his face. "No worries, Benji," he said. "I'm enjoying the fresh air. Hello, Rachel."

"Hello, sir."

"Just call me George. I'm glad to see you're hitting it off with my grandson. He's quite the fellow."

"I should probably take Grandpa back," Benji said to Rachel. "May I... may I call you sometime?"

Several heartbeats passed before she smiled. "Sure, I guess."

"Uh, your number?"

"Your stepmother has it." She smiled.

Benji waved and walked down the path. As soon as he got into the ubr, his grandfather turned to him.

George said, "Something makes me want to ask you your intentions. Rachel seems like someone nice. Someone who deserves to know the truth."

"Thanks for not trumping me, Grandpa." Benji sighed. "The truth is that Mary and I had a big fight. I... I'll go and end things with her today." He swallowed. It wouldn't be easy.

George nodded. "Sorry to hear about you and Mary."

"Catherine never liked her much."

"Catherine and Irene both have your best interests at heart, Benji. As do I."

They rode on in silence for a while. Then Benji put his hand on his grandfather's arm. "Grandpa," he said. "I was wondering if you could tell me sometime about what life was like when you were younger."

"You're interested?"

Benji nodded.

"I'm thinking that I'd like to create a documentary from your stories."

George slowly smiled. "Would you like to come in and listen while I take my medicine?"

Benji smiled back. "Yes, I think I would." His mind filled with images of what his project would be like, with original footage interspersed with archival film and his grandfather's voice-overs. "Would it be okay if I recorded what you say?"

"I guess so."

"Thanks, Grandpa."

Make The World A Better Place

PH Johannesen

Lewis's tablet was distracting - the screen had the words *A Better Place* flashing across it. It was part of the mission statement of the program under his leadership as Director. Avoiding the child in front of him, his eyes scanned the room. It was a simple classroom converted into a dojo with mirrors lining one wall and padding on the floor. He reluctantly shifted his glance back to to Lisa, a small ten-year-old girl who was looking up at him with large brown eyes and a pouty lip.

"I'm sorry Lisa, you have to take your karate class today. You have no choice in the matter," he said.

"But I want to read. Both you and Margaret said that reading was good for me!" Lisa's lip was trembling.

"Yes, but you need to keep up on your sports too. And that book is fiction, not the history book we were talking about," Lewis sighed heavily. "Give me the book, you'll be allowed to have it back at dinner."

Lisa threw the book at his head, then stalked out onto the floor of the dojo with four other children. Subjects, Lewis would correct his co-workers when they spoke. They were subjects, not children. She was the oldest subject in the program.

Lewis rolled his eyes as he caught the book and put it on a chair. When he took this job, he had not intended to become a parent figure. It had been left out of the job description. Perhaps the government thought it was implied. When you genetically engineer children, someone will have to take the parent role.

"You got her out there?" Margaret, his equal rank, walked up to him, frowning at the five children who were stretching, "I had to promise Eriona an extra hour of cello practice tonight instead of homework to get her out there. Adam threw a fit too. Says that he's against all forms of violence as a whole. I had to convince him that martial arts aren't about fighting."

"Well, they're not normally," Lewis said.

"But we're teaching them to actually fight," Margaret said, "And these are smart kids, they're picking up on that."

"Have they had outside contact again?" Lewis asked.

"Since Ava hacked the network from her handheld game system?" Margaret asked, "No, not that we're aware of." Lewis looked carefully at the five children. Ava was six, the youngest of first group. She deftly landed an incredibly powerful punch on the instructor's mitt and he reeled backwards.

"Maybe the next batch will be easier to control," he muttered. He was referring to the second half of the experiment, the five remaining children- all under five years of age. They were learning from the older group that they needed to restrict music, literature, and art, making sure to surround them with toy soldiers instead of paint brushes.

"Whatever makes you sleep at night?" Margaret said dryly.

Lewis walked with his boss's boss's boss, William, as the first five children were eating lunch, and joined Margaret in observing them. The children were allowed to eat together in a small cafeteria so they could learn basic social skills and fit in while on reconnaissance or assassination missions.

"Will you do me a Favor please Eriona And pass the salt now!" Fred called. Eriona passed it to him.

"My gratitude for
the favor you have bestowed

to me with the salt."

"What is that boy doing?" William asked.

"I think he's speaking in haiku. That's Fred, he's obsessed with poetry. He'll only speak in some form of poetry half the time. Last week it was limericks. He had half the staff needing to leave to laugh." Margaret offered, "We think that's how he keeps himself challenged."

"You mean, subject number 4?" William was checking his notes, "Why are they studying poetry? How will that help them when they're in the military as our super-human weapons?"

"We're giving them a whole education. It could help them blend in if they end up undercover," Lewis stated blandly, "but in general it was decided that they need at least a high school education level to be competent, but since all have tested IQs at genius or higher level, we've raised the bar to college. This whole group is roughly Senior year in college in most subjects."

"Well, clearly you're teaching them too much." William said.

"We allow them to study their personal interests as rewards for good behavior and for studying the parts of our program they don't like." Lewis replied.

"Well, clearly you're giving them too much opportunity for self expression. I want more physical training. Start them running basic military training regimes." William snapped.

"Ava's only nine, it's a little young to start military regimes that are meant for grown men," Margaret said aghast.

"Subject number 5? Yes. She can still start running them," William walked away, "Let me see the progress for the younger set."

"Leave me alone, I'm writing," Lisa had locked herself in her room. She was now seventeen, nearing the end of the planned training time. The plan was for her to enter the military as a special agent on her eighteenth birthday, but she was making that difficult by fighting against all training that did not involve reading and writing.

"We can unlock the door, you do realize that?" Lewis called. He felt exhausted. The program was well into its 22nd year- five for developing the DNA for each child, and seventeen with actual living humans. Although a young man when it started, Lewis felt like he had aged quickly and was easily frustrated now. None of the subjects were taking to their training well. Lisa was outright fighting them on it, and as the oldest she was bringing the rest of her group with her in protest. Even the younger group was catching on - infected by the belligerence more and more as they all became young adults, rather than little children.

Even Josh, the youngest of them all, and the most adept at hand to hand combat, was quickly catching Lisa's ideals and using them to manipulate dance classes out of Lewis and Margaret.

"I built a better lock," Lisa shouted back at him, "go ahead and try!"

"You have to go to combat class. It's not an option, Lisa." Lewis said firmly.

"Only for two more months, then I'm eighteen!" Lisa finally opened the door to shout it in his face.

"Then you'll have an actual drill sergeant to answer to!" Lewis said loudly, barely holding onto his cool.

"We'll see about that!" Lisa yelled.

Lewis winced as William yelled loudly enough to rival rock concert decibels, "What do you mean, only three children remain in the program?"

"Adam left to join the Peace Corps," Margaret said calmly, "And Ava, she's working to fight cyber bullying. She said that it was far more important than what we were trying to make her do."

"I wonder how she got that idea," William glared at Margaret.

"That's uncalled for, with all due respect sir." Lewis cut in, "We've worked hard these last thirty years to raise these children to be your super soldiers, and have always towed the line. We just never cracked the genetic code for getting them to obey orders well enough."

"That's nurtured behavior! Not natured!" William shouted. Lewis shrugged, and walked over to the window overlooking where the last three subjects were enjoying a brief free time outside in the courtyard. Josh, the youngest, was working on a dance, some combination of hip-hop and ballet, to a song on an iPod he must have convinced a staff member to lend him. Sam was building something out of trash. Lewis was not sure if it was functional or art, perhaps it was both. Lydia was lying there seeing things in the clouds.

"Those three better work out!" William bellowed. Lewis opened his mouth to voice his doubts, but remembered who he was talking to just in time. He looked over to Margaret. She was watching Josh, with a concerned look on her face. They both knew they were down to three chances.

"Well, it's officially over, I guess we failed," Lewis sat down at the cafe with Margaret.

"Oh?" She asked.

"Building a better human. Someone ready to fight for the world and defend us. They're not funding us for the future since all ten washed out. We got the official decree today. We failed." He honestly was not surprised. It had been five years since Josh had left the program to try his hand at acting. They kept doing paperwork in the meantime, waiting for clearance to engineer more children.

Margaret glanced down at the news article she was reading. The photo showed a filmier face— Subject #10, little Josh. Now only 23 years old and a star. The headline said "Film and Broadway Star Builds Tuition-Free After School Theatre Center for New York's Youth!" The article linked to another, "Famous Cellist Eriona Connects Youth From 60 Countries in Free Festival!". Another, "Author Lisa wins Pulitzer in Fiction. Donates Profits to At-Risk Youth." Another, "Rapper Fred Defends Travel to Korea for Performances- Says Music Brings the World Together". It did not take much searching to find similar headlines for all ten children.

"The directive was to create people to help make the world a better place. I'm not so sure we failed," Margaret smiled, showing Lewis the news.

Once Upon A Time Again

Gregory Wright

"Stupid fingers," Joseph muttered in disgust at his reflection in the mirror. "Worthless."

"Need help with the tie, Dad?" his son chimed in.

"No!" he replied with a sudden exasperated exhale.

Silently, his son slipped up behind him, reached over his shoulders and looked at the task at hand in the mirror.

When father and son were placed together, their resemblance was muted but acceptable. The old man was now eighty-six while the son was a healthy fifty-three. While the son expertly folded and creased the fabric into a neat thick bowtie, the father studied the man's expression and smiled at the resemblance he had to his wife, features that he could clearly ascertain.

"You really look like your mother the older you get."

The son smiled. "Is that the real reason you want me around so much?" The father shrugged and smiled. "You're useful in other ways too, Max."

It was easy to compare the deep lines of age in his own face with those just beginning in his son. But what made him smile were the eyes, the high cheekbones and the dimpled chin that Max had gotten from Emily, his mother.

"There!" Max exclaimed, then patted his father firmly on the back. "I did it double thick, just the way you like it."

"Just like I taught you." Joseph said with a smile.

"I believe it was Mom."

"Oh, that's right. I forgot."

"Just because she isn't here to defend herself, doesn't mean she isn't here."

"Speaking of isn't here, where are your sisters?"

"Catherine will meet us at the church because your granddaughter..."

"Which one?"

His son gave him a knowing look.

"Oh, Abby again."

"...has decided the dress she was supposed to wear wasn't what she was in the mood for."

"Catherine was the same way at eight. Payback's a bitch."

"And Jessica will be here momentarily, because she is Jessica."

"Well, at least you're here," he said disgruntled.

"Thanks, Dad." Max replied.

The father turned around slowly and gazed around the bedroom as if for the last time. The wallpaper was colored in yellow and red roses, long vines pulling the flowers together in laced green lines. The tall ceiling of the room gave the feeling of more room than there was, as the antique oaken dressers filled in the corners. A heavy oak bed frame with tall posts on the corners dominated the center. Covering the bed was a patched quilt, adding even more color to the room. Tall thin windows facing the west brought in abundant afternoon light, its beams gracing the thick yellow area rug on the floor.

On the night stand nearest the mirror, there was an old, yellowed picture of a very young man and a beautiful young woman, she in his arms, each smiling in the pleasure of the moment. Smiling back at it, Joseph stared in remembrance. Max responded to a noise at the door which gave him the excuse to leave the room. "I'll get that," he yelled back to no one in particular as he quickly left the bedroom.

Joseph slowly walked around the bedroom. Gazing at the pictures of the kids, now grown. Relatives long past. Some he liked. Other pictures he truly wanted to forget, but being mostly on Emily's side of the family, couldn't remove due to a promise he made to her. Hence the stuffed monkey in front of his mother in law's picture. Fitting, he thought.

Reaching the other side of the bed, he picked up a picture solely of Emily on a bench in the woods. He loved this picture more than any other as it was a perfect scene, a cool fall day with a clear blue sky, and a background of yellow and red maple leaves falling all around her. It was the perfect place in their lives also. He had accepted a position at a new architecture firm. His future looked to be promising and successful with the children: Jessica the youngest was four, Catherine eleven, and Max was in the middle at six. No babies, but young enough to enjoy.

He placed his hand over Emily's face, and closed his eyes. Dreaming again, as if willing himself to feel her touch. "I miss you, Emily," he said, then replaced the picture on the night stand, and softly left the room. Closing the door, he then adjusted his collar, straightened the tie, and walked down the narrow wooden staircase of the hundred-year-old home, leading to the first floor. Placed along the wall leading to the main floor were pictures of the kids at various ages along with pictures of homes and office buildings he had designed and built.

A montage of their life together, he glanced at them all as he progressed down each step.

Reaching the main floor, he stared at the mess that had suddenly appeared. There Jessica had her coat on the floor, her shoes off to the side and her purse on the ground next to her, dominating all of the space with her presence. Joseph smiled. That was Jessica.

She hesitated amongst the chaos she was creating. "Wow, Dad, you look great!'

He smiled. "Thank you."

Examining the baggage, she had brought, he pulled the bottom of his tuxedo down to straighten out the front, and smiled broadly. "Glad you could make it."

"Wouldn't miss it," she replied

She then tossed her hair back, while reaching into her purse to draw out a brush. Turning away from him, she stood in front of the hall mirror and in quick movements began to brush out her hair, quickly brushed away some fabric off her brilliant red dress, then reached up and adjusted her breasts so they were even.

"Don't work so hard," Max said, entering the foyer from the kitchen with a glass of sherry in a small, clear tumbler. "It's just family."

"Just because you and Catherine are married with kids doesn't mean I have to look frumpy. Besides, the reception is in the hotel downtown. Lots of opportunity."

She turned and faced her much taller brother. "Where is your beautiful bride and 'the boy' "?

"She will meet us at the church. She is helping Catherine with her four girls. We got a call early this morning requesting back up. 'The boy' went with because it was going to be boring here."

Jessica glanced over her shoulder and seeing that her father was distracted by something in the living room, she leaned in towards Max. "This is such a waste of time and money," she said with a hiss. She glanced back again to be sure the coast was clear, then continued, "I could have had Bowie hologram concert tickets."

Max leaned in towards her. "Really? See, I honestly think you're angry that this isn't about you."

She scowled and returned to her prep work. Max grinned and took another sip.

Looking at the pictures of the grandchildren in the living room, Joseph smiled at the thought of all his grandchildren together. Four girls and one boy. Hence 'the boy,' no name necessary. Good kids all of them. They were Emily's pride.

Outside a car horn honked, and Max opened the front door to a beautiful, cool, spring morning and a long, thin, black limousine parked on the street in front. "Couldn't ask for a better day," he said, as he chucked down the last swallow of sherry, placed the glass on the mantle of the coat rack near the door, and helped his father navigate around the mess that was Jessica.

As they walked down the front steps, he heard Jessica suddenly fumble and begin the descent behind them. By habit, Joseph stopped and looked back at the house, gazing at the second-storey window where their bedroom was. For so many years he had done this. In the beginning, watching a young bride waving goodbye, later with children on her hip, and in the last days, when she had the strength, with the oxygen tank by her side and the hoses leading up to her nose. Weakly waving goodbye as he went to the office.

"Ready, Dad?" Max said as he opened the rear door. While he stood there, Jessica passed by like a city bus, and leapt into the limo. Joseph flush with the memory, looked away and entered the car, the door behind him closing.

The limousine drove quickly to the church. Being on a Saturday morning with perfect weather, there was little traffic, and Joseph lowered the window to enjoy the breeze and the fresh air. Arriving at the church, all the missing participants were standing in front of the church, the children wrestling and elbowing as the adults struggled to keep them well-behaved and looking their best at the same time. Joseph came out after Jessica, followed closely by Max. Catherine trotted down the white limestone steps of the cathedral and kissed Joseph lightly on the cheek.
"We're so excited for you, Dad."

He could only smile and nod. The event was beginning to be real now, after months of planning. Surrounding him was the church and only his family, nothing could be better. Feeling a little weak from anxiety, he began the ascent up the stairs and through the heavy oaken doors of the church. Behind him, he could hear the children chattering, the youngest girl speaking in a hoarse whisper. "But where's Grandma?"

"I will explain it to you once we get into the church," was the harsh reply.

Joseph halted in front of the waiting crowd. "Good question Charlotte." He replied. "How about I explain this to you now?" When Max and Jessica had joined the group, Joseph held out his arms as if in a group hug. "I means so much to me that you are all here. I understand that there were some concerns." He glanced at Jessica. She crossed her arms and rolled her eyes, looking away defensively. "But I want you to understand. All of you are here because of what happened on a day just like today. This family. The ones I love more than anything in this world." He hesitated dropping his arms. "Your mother died eighteen months ago. I promised her that on our fiftieth wedding anniversary, we would renew our vows. Not for us. We loved each other every hour of every day. But for you. Because it was this was the greatest moment from our marriage that we could share. I want you to see how beautiful your mother was, and why this was the greatest day of our lives, and because there is always hope, even with her absence." He stopped there, the emotion catching him.

There was a silence, then Max slipped away to enter the church to finalize the details. The rest of the family shuffled in soon after. As the family entered the church, their destination being the front pews, Joseph halted at the entrance to the gallery. Around them the soft sound of the organ filled the empty space while the soloist punctuated the air with notes as she warmed up.

Standing alone, Joseph revisited his motives, constantly shifting from 'this is crazy' to 'I always want to remember this day.' Up in the corners of the rectory he could see the white lenses of the cameras, crossing at the appropriate angles to give the best views. Looking at the altar, he could see the tall vases with thick branches of rhododendron and forsythia showing their spring plumage. Rhododendrons were Emily's favorite. 'She'll be pleased,' he thought.

Max came out of a side room, slightly disheveled with concern, but confident. He quickly approached his father, a technician following him close behind, earpieces in both ears, microphone in place, monitor on his belt. They quickly clustered around Joseph and filled him in on the details.

"We are ready," the technician said, fine white teeth shining through a well-trimmed red beard. "We did a number of practice runs, and there were a few glitches, which we worked out. I mean, the disk you gave us was pretty old, but we were able to draw out what we needed." He reached into his shirt pocket and pulled out a thin red zip drive. Placing it in Joseph's hand, Joseph then slid it into his pocket for safekeeping.

"Are we all set then?" Max asked.

Joseph took a deep shaky breath. Thinking about replying, he instead just shook his head, a lock of white hair, slipping over his eyebrow.

Raising a small microphone on his collar the technician mumbled something and then turned to look behind them. On cue, a woman about Emily's height and build emerged from a nearby anteroom, followed by another technician.

She was dressed oddly. Wearing a bright orange body suit that covered her head to toe, with small purple balls, each the size of a dime all over her suit, with scarcely an inch between them. Across her face, the same small balls were glued directly to her skin so her entire figure was covered. Joseph winced a little, wondering how this would all play out. Max, sensing his father's doubts, reached over and grasped Joseph's tricep in support. By instinct, Joseph reached over and grasped his son's hand.

Motioning with two fingers, the technician led the young woman to a spot at the entrance to the galley. She stood there motionless, as straight as possible, as the technician centered her in middle of the aisle. When he was convinced everything was in place, he stepped back and motioned for Joseph to stand beside the young woman. Following the instructions, Joseph did as he was directed, standing awkwardly next to the pixelated teenager.

The technician stood back and paused. "Advance," he said quietly into the microphone.

Suddenly the woman next to Joseph was enveloped in a haze, meshed light blurring her features until suddenly the image of a young woman blurred out the suit and the occupant in it. A beautiful young woman appeared, dressed in a dated wedding dress, her shocking blue eyes lit up with wonder and hope.

Joseph gasped. Max was speechless and the technician smiled. Whispering more directions and encouragement to the people behind the scenes.

"Emily!" Joseph whispered hoarsely.

"Grandma!" the children squealed. Catherine sniffed and wiped her eyes, while Jessica stood stunned.

It was true. It was her, dressed exactly like she had been on their wedding day, the image pulled from an old tape of the original ceremony, reconstructed and placed next to Joseph.

"I've missed you," Joseph said, tearing up. The model could only nod, so as not to give the illusion away, but Joseph was already overwhelmed knowing that his wife was here once more. "I always said I would marry you again," he added. He held out his elbow as the pastor approached the altar, the soloist began to sing, and his wife looped her arm in his to walk down the aisle once again.

Step Right In

Debra Kollar

Angela Garrett sat by herself on a white backless sofa waiting to be healed at The New Psychology Freedom Center. She kept her distance from the rest. She was the only one who was court ordered to receive treatment, because of her suicide attempt. There were fifty in her group, standing around chattering underneath the dome of the atrium, like caged birds anticipating their release back out into the world. The center's slogan: *Be pain free! Live your best life! Be happy all the time!*

They had attended the Meet and Greet Party held a week ago. They all shared one theme: the death of a child. After an hour, it had become a soireé for the depressed. The center had not factored in that there were only so many death stories people could hear in one night.

Angela had left the function early that evening, after the born-again blonde with the sunny disposition—*It's Suzie with a Z!*—had introduced herself, assuring Angela that the death of her daughter, Stella, was all part of God's plan. *Isn't it nice to know your child resides in the glorious Kingdom of God?* Angela wished she had screamed at the woman, "My daughter most certainly does not belong in heaven. She belongs here with me playing hopscotch on the pavement of schoolyards, licking the sides of melting ice cream cones—being alive!"

She spotted Suzie on the other side of the waiting room conducting prayer circles in her "What Would Jesus Do?" printed T-Shirt.

It's a facade. The whole damn thing. The more Angela looked around, the more she realized everything appeared to be *off*—the plush white sofas without backs to sit comfortably, the Berber carpet with heavier loops made for foot traffic, purchased in an unforgiving cream-color, a wall decorated with gilded portraits of the smiling faces of happy satisfied patients. Yet, here in this room happiness could not to be found—*well, except for Suzie.*

In the middle of the atrium stood a garish black display case, parting the group like Moses had parted the Red Sea. Whether it was from its crooked legs or the nefarious looking objects housed inside it, no one would socialize nearby.

Nine surreal sculptures of individuals molded into contorted and twisted shapes lay atop the shelves. The first was of a woman in a firm stance, her mouth open and screaming. The next one, androgynous in nature, pulled at its form in protest. The sculpture in the middle was of a man on his knees, raising his head and hands toward the sky praying—pleading—for God to do something. All nine looked as if they were in horrific agony, an interpretation vaguely reminding her of Dante's Inferno and the nine circles of hell.

A portrait painter by trade, art was in her blood as thick as the depression that plagued her. The statues affected her in ways she could not understand.

She pressed the scar on her left wrist with her right index finger. The serpentine line reminded her of a past she could not escape. She had stopped scraping and digging at it, in an attempt at self-control. Occasionally, she would revert, using the pain to keep her rooted in the present, trying not to fall into the despair caused by Stella's death.

Now the judge would not let her escape either. Court ordered to receive treatment or be a permanent resident in one of the few remaining psychiatric facilities, her choices were limited. With The New Psychology Freedom Center in existence, the government and medical community would not give any sympathy to suicide attempts.

"Miss Garrett?"

A lanky man stood over by the only door leading into the main building. His wrinkled gray sport coat clashed with his silk Hawaiian button-down, giving her the impression it had been pulled out from the bottom drawer of his desk. The gloomy color and poor fit reminded Angela of mornings in Seattle, the gray haze never completely giving way to the sunshine.

"My name is Kal. I'm here to do your intake."

She glanced back at the group for support. Everyone had stopped talking and was looking her way. Some were clearly excited. Others looked at her nervously, hoping the place she would be going was safe, because soon they would be going too. Suzie placed her hand to her heart and tilted her head to the side, tearing up like a proud mother sending off one of her children to college. They all expected to leave this center pain free. She thought of Stella, her beautiful raven-haired girl, and walked through the door, unsure of what lay beyond.

Angela followed the man down the hallway and tried to focus on his introductory speech, not wanting to think of Stella.

He had a short bleached-blonde ponytail, tied high, revealing a shaved lower back head with the words LOOK UP tattooed on the nape of his neck. She was about to ask what it meant, and what would have compelled a person to get a tattoo only others could see, when they stopped.

"Right here, to the left. The viewing room," he announced. "Please take a seat."

Angela walked inside surprised to see more white backless sofas identical to the ones in the atrium. "What did you do? Buy these in bulk?"

Kal fussed with the video remote, oblivious to her remark. "So, you have a short presentation to watch. I'll be back after it's over."

A silver-haired man in a lab coat popped up on the screen. He looked past the camera as if he was receiving direction from someone. "I'm Doctor Kenneth Fenway, a founding member of The New Psychology Freedom Center. Welcome to the Limbic Synapse Rerouting System Chamber Unit."

"Wow, that's a mouthful." Angela said.

The camera panned over a glossy green-colored pod placed horizontally on the ground with the hatch opened. Fenway explained that they designed the chambers to be shaped like chrysalises, the hard outer cases left behind after caterpillars turned into butterflies. He talked of the combined benefits of technology and science. "Remember, we are the future in mind and body wellness," he said at the end.

Angela waited as credits played to Michael Jackson's *Heal the World*.

Kal walked back into the viewing room. "You've gotta love corporate videos. Fortunately for you, it's the monkeys who run this facility," he grinned.

"I noticed."

"Come with me."

Angela followed him into his office and stopped when she saw the wall behind Kal's desk. "Wow!"

She had become a portrait artist to paint on canvas the positive emotions that she did not feel. Because of this, she knew every shade of acrylic paint. The wall was covered with brilliant colored butterflies—sun yellows, cobalt blues, lime tree greens, magentas and violets—flying away from a bed of foliage and flowers with delicate hanging, moss-colored cocoons. "Who painted the mural? It's breathtaking."

"A former patient and friend of mine. To symbolize the transformation the patients go through." Kal pointed to the bottom of the mural where lush vegetation was painted in shades of gray. "Caterpillars only see life in shades of light and dark." He pointed higher. "They emerge as butterflies and see the world in color."

"If only it were that easy," she sighed.

"Oh, but it is. Do you see the good looking blue butterfly closest to the sun? That's me," he winked. "She painted it to remind me of how hard I've worked to get back to the sunlight."

"You were a patient?" Angela said, surprised.

"I was a top-rated climbing instructor before I was recruited for the war in the Middle East. I came home with PTSD. It was pretty horrible. I stopped climbing entirely. Otherwise, I would've jumped off the top to feel free for thirty seconds."

Angela wondered if she had misjudged the man with the bleached-blond ponytail.

Kal sat down behind his desk. "So what are your questions?"

"How long would I sleep?"

"Well, it depends."

"Depends on what?" Angela did not like vague replies. They were used too often by doctors who did not know the answers.

"On what ails you."

"On what ails me? What kind of answer is that? Let's see, Bob," Angela said, acting it out. "This one here," she pointed at herself, "needs an extra few days in the chamber to get rid of suicidal tendencies. In fact, better add in an extra week just to be safe."

"Look. It depends on how many issues you want resolved. If you want to replace bad issues with good feelings or erase them all together. Technically, it's one night. Give or take a few hours."

"A full night? Just like that?"

"As easy as that," Kal smiled.

Angela looked at the photo of a chamber unit on his desk. "They look like hibernation pods in sci-fi movies," she observed. "You're not warehousing us as food, are you? For when you fly back to your home world." She smiled weakly.

"No, this is not some science fiction movie." He shook his head, the slightest smile coming across his face. "The chamber units are basically beds." He pulled out a contraption that looked like a futuristic halo. "This does the magic. Your emotions and memories are contained in the limbic region of your brain. It simply reroutes the synapses, creating new memories for your past experiences and changes your emotional response to painful memories. There is a lot this little device can do."

Angela turned it over and felt a kind of anxiety that comes with being restrained. *What if something went wrong and made me worse?*

She pushed it toward him. "I don't think this is for me." She caught herself pressing her right index finger into the scar on her left wrist again.

At the start of this process, Angela had hope. Now though, she imagined that the process would not only abduct her memories of Stella, but take away her identity.

"You should meet with my colleague, Kathleen, before you cancel. At this point, what do you have to lose?" Kal brought her to an office at the end of the hallway.

She saw Kathleen's title on the door. "You're bringing me to a psychologist?"

"Oh, she's more than a psychologist. Please sit down and I'll go find Kathleen."

Angela remembered as a young girl sitting with her father in the hallway of the emergency room on a wooden bench, staring at a pale green wall muddled with grime and fingerprints, while medical personnel rushed her mother beyond the automated doors marked "Authorized Personnel Only."

She and her father had sat there quietly, knowing the inevitable had happened. Her mother had succeeded. It had been her third try; it had been only a matter of time. She had finally swallowed the right combination of pills—and enough of them—to insure the doctor's could not bring her back this time.

"Human beings have a need to fix broken things," her father had told her. "But sometimes, they can't be fixed."

Angela's depression had started during her thirteenth year. Little by little, she forgot what normal had felt like. Despite the medications and the therapy through the years, she would never feel like an active participant in the world again; always on the outside looking in.

The psychiatrists sent her home with copious amounts of medications; pills the color of jelly beans. Some helped, others made her suicidal. Trying to find the right mix and then hoping the relief would stay.

Just like with her mother, though, it was impossible to control, so difficult to not let it invade her world. With time, she was managing it, until God had given her another tragedy.

She remembered how Non-Hodgkin Lymphoma was not an easy group of words to pronounce. How could a child have cancer? She had tried to convince the doctor he had made a mistake, but he was just the jury, delivering the information. The sentence had already been passed, and it would be final. There would be no second chance. Like any illness, Angela had learned to say and explain it on a daily basis, to doctors, to friends, to a four-year-old child who did not understand why she was in so much pain.

No matter how she had tried to control her depression, she simply could not handle both it and Stella's death together.

A woman with peachy-colored flamingos dangling from her earlobes charged into the office. "Hi, hon. I'm Kathleen."

Kathleen was even more atypical to this place than Kal had been. Her wide-leg Palazzo lounge pants were long for her short frame; although, not long enough to hide the pink Croc clogs she was wearing. Angela wondered if everything in this building was a smoke and mirrors set-up and the true nature was hidden. The sculptures, Kal's ponytail, the butterfly mural, Kathleen's shoes, were unseen unless someone paid attention.

Angela moved around in her seat to get comfortable while Kathleen searched for a pen. She did not know why Kal thought this woman could change her mind.

"Oh, here it is." She held up a glittery pen with the pink breast cancer awareness ribbon on it. "We're all survivors here in some shape or form." She began to write something down and then looked up. "So, Kal tells me you're hesitant about the program. What seems to be the problem?"

"There isn't a problem. I don't think this is for me." Angela tugged at the cuffs of her blouse.

Kathleen pointed her pen toward Angela's wrists. "How long have you had those?"

"Two years." She folded her hands inside of her lap.

"After Stella died?"

"After Stella died," Angela replied.

Kathleen went back to writing in her notes. "So why *don't* you want to do this, hon?"

"I don't have the time," Angela answered.

Kathleen looked up and smirked, "Chicken shit."

"Chicken what?" Angela wondered if this woman had been a patient, too, with a diagnosis of crazy.

Kathleen challenged her. "A night of healing to replace a lifetime of hurting? It's a no brainer."

"And I don't want to lose who I am," Angela added.

"Chicken shit," Kathleen replied.

"Cut it out! You know about my mother, right?" Angela did not wait for a response. The rage and heartbreak she had tried to keep hidden was being unleashed. "Nobody helped my mom—nobody! They said they would, they made promises, but they didn't. She couldn't be there for me, and I couldn't be there for Stella. So why should I get a free ride? Two broken people, my parents, gave birth to a very broken child. That child grew up and then had another child who was broken. Everybody's broken in my family. Oh, and dead too by the way. That's my lineage. That's *my* story."

Unrelenting, Kathleen shook her head. "Nope, you're playing the victim because it's the only thing you've known. You have a cure and it scares you. Who would Angela Garrett be without pain riding her back? The answer: the real you. You'd be free. Hell, look at Kal. He's back to climbing 15,000 foot mountains for God's sake!"

"I'm not Kal. And a mountain isn't going to bring back my daughter."

"Think Angela! Would your mother—and everything *she* had to go through—want you to pass up this opportunity? Would you not have done anything to give your child, Stella, a cure if one was available? Don't you owe it to them to be saved?"

Angela thought about how her mother had begged the psychiatrists to give her something to take away her manic episodes. How she had Stella pinned and pricked with every treatment available; taking the four-year-old to see specialists when Stella had wanted to spend her last days at home. Kathleen was right. She owed it to her mother; she owed it to her little girl who did not receive another option. "I'll do it," she whispered.

"Then let's go, hon," Kathleen squirmed her body out from the desk chair. "Time's a ticking if we want to get this done today." She stopped from gathering her paperwork to impart the importance of what Angela was about to undertake. "Each day we receive more requests from people wanting to be healed. You're one of the lucky ones. Please remember that."

As they walked back to Kal's office, Angela stopped by a table of ceramic projects painted by kids. There were lopsided pots, cinched bowls and hand-built animals. "Art is all around this place."

"Art heals the soul," Kathleen answered.

"I wanted to ask you. Those sculptures in the waiting room, what are they about? Is it Dante's Inferno and the nine circles of hell?"

"Not Dante's Inferno, but you could call it hell."

"I don't understand?" Angela remembered the tormented faces of the people. Hard to look at, hard to turn away from.

"They are the objects which stand out strangely—and singularly—in an otherwise, beautiful room. They represent how the mentally ill, the outsiders and the broken-hearted feel in a normal society. Each piece is about suffering—hearing voices, not being able to leave the house, being born in the wrong body, losing a child. You see?"

"But this center is a healing place. Why show art that reminds people of their pain?" Angela asked.

"Do you know Max Clement?" Kathleen said proudly.

"Yes, of course." Angela knew of him well. The famous sculptor's pieces were everywhere: in museums, the White House, art galleries in New York City.

"He sculpted the pieces for the founding members to show in art what pain feels like to someone who doesn't have a way to escape it. Mr. Clement had some kind of extreme anxiety and OCD—it's public knowledge. Now he's cured."

"I would've never guessed he had a mental illness." Angela remembered seeing Clement's sculpture in The Louvre on an art trip to Paris. A bronze statue of a boy holding the sun in his hands. *La Joie De Vivre*—The Joy of Living.

"Many artists have mental illnesses," Kathleen reminded her. "You never know what goes on in a person's mind. The same goes for the famous, intelligent, wealthy, or otherwise. No one gets a free pass in this world. And now we've arrived. She's good to go, Kal," she said stopping in the doorway of his office.

"I knew with you, she would be." Kal gave her a wave of thanks before Kathleen disappeared down the hallway.

Fifteen minutes later, after documents were reviewed and signed, a nurse arrived to take Angela to what they referred to as the sleeping warehouse. The nurse brought Angela to a room to change into a white, cotton shirt and pant set.

The sleeping warehouse was massive. A hundred or so sleeping chambers lined in rows as far as Angela could see. "So many sad people to treat," she said in disbelief.

The nurse replied, "Heal not treat. This is the difference between traditional psychiatry and us."

"Exactly," a familiar voice said.

Angela turned to see Kal behind her.

"I thought it would be good for you to see a friendly face as you fell asleep. I know it sounds sentimental, but Kathleen and I tend to sympathize with those who have to climb the farthest." He turned around and pointed to the two words tattooed on the back of his neck. LOOK UP. "This means to look up and fight for that beautiful sunlight."

She understood now why his tattoo was on the back of his neck where others could see it. She thought about the blue butterfly on the wall of

Kal's office, closest to the sun. He was already in the sunlight, enjoying life again. He wanted to show others, they could too.

"We're ready, Miss Garrett." The nurse looked at her clipboard. "I have the paperwork with the ailments you listed at your initial consultation. I just need last minute confirmations on what you would like done with them."

"Okay." She felt nervous. She reached for the scar on her wrist and decided to clasp her hands together instead.

"Anxiety?" The nurse looked at Angela.

"Take it away," Angela replied.

"Low self-esteem?"

Angela hesitated.

"I can make you think you look like a model?" The nurse offered.

"Will I *look* like a model?"

"The chamber units don't change your physical appearance," the nurse said. "Science hasn't evolved far enough. Although, I'm the first in line when they can make me look like the supermodel Danielle Vegas," she winked.

"Can you replace it with confidence instead?"

"Sure. What about your depression?"

Angela looked down at the scars on her wrists. "Take it away completely."

"The last one. I'm sorry. Stella's death?"

Angela remembered writing her daughter's name on the ailment sheet at the initial doctor's appointment. Curving the top and bottom of the letter S, looping the lowercase l's in solid black ink. She did not intend to list her as an ailment. Stella, named after her grandmother, Angela's mother, couldn't live past the age of four in the world. She had thought this time the name Stella would be strong, that it could have a happy ending, a permanence in some form in life. It was not meant to be.

"That one I want to keep." Angela wanted to remember every moment with her daughter. "But can you add acceptance and self-forgiveness for those memories?"

"Consider it done. Anything else?"

"No, I'm ready."

"Step right in, Miss Garrett." Kal stood over by the chamber, holding his hand out to assist her. "I'll be here tomorrow after your transformation. Maybe, I'll even let you paint yourself into my mural as a little pink butterfly," he winked.

The nurse situated the programmed halo on top of Angela's head and pressed the button for the chamber to close.

She realized for the first time, she was not afraid.

She had become an artist to make joyful, colorful art, to visually see what she could not feel. When she would wake up tomorrow, her life would not be muted with the black thick despair of her depression, the gray endless days of sadness without her daughter.

Closing her eyes, she waited for what they had told her would be the best sleep of her life. To be transformed, to become alive, hopeful, present, to feel for the first time what life would be like in color. She dreamed, first in shades of light and dark and then in beautiful, vivid colors. At the end, transformed into a butterfly, she flapped her wings, slowly then fiercely, and flew toward the sunlight, free.

Paulie

Bonnie B. Bradlee

Every molecule of air seemed to shimmer with the eerie glow that came from nowhere, and from everywhere. Jason, a seasoned meteorologist, had seen many strange atmospheric conditions, but never anything like this. His thoughts swirled as much as the snow, which blew in ever changing patterns across the great prairie. He shouted into the vast nothingness, "What am I doing out here? Why did I come out here looking for you? Paulie, why did you leave the way you did? And that note! What's up with that note?"

Paulie had disappeared a few weeks earlier, leaving an obscure note saying, "I go to seek a Great Perhaps." Under normal circumstances Jason wouldn't have bothered. If his nephew wanted to leave, let him leave, he's of age. But circumstances were not normal. When he did a search of the words in Paulie's note, Jason found that they were the last words of the 16th century French Renaissance writer, François Rabelais, and that made it sound like a suicide note. But he knew that Paulie would never do that, not now. Sure there had been a time when suicide would have been the obvious answer to such a disappearance, but that was the past. Paulie had worked through everything after giving his life to the Lord. He even got a semicolon tattoo to raise awareness for mental health, depression, and suicide prevention awareness. The semicolon, he'd said, signified that his sentence wasn't finished yet, there was more to come. This was not a suicide.

Jason, not just uncle, but mentor, walking with Paulie as he cleaned himself up, had taken the matter into his own hands when the police refused to investigate. They said that they didn't have time to go chasing after every down and out addict who fell off the wagon and wandered into the vast prairie to die. And so he prayed, night after night, pleading for answers, questioning, letting his desires be known. The desire to know what happened, what Paulie did or didn't do - was he dead or alive, or hurt somewhere, or kidnapped, or did he just take off? So many questions, so many prayers, and the only answer he heard was, "Go find out for yourself." It was strange, but he felt compelled to pursue it. So he left home and comfort, friends and family, to find his nephew and to know, once and for all, what happened.

Now he was halfway across the prairie, the huge expanse of nothingness that lay to the west of civilization. It was greater than the greatest ocean, like a barrier to the edge of forever. No one knew what lay on the other side of the prairie. Though many had ventured out, no one had ever returned. And it was here, in the middle of this vastness that Jason encountered the eerie, supernatural, effervescent light. He stopped in his tracks, examining the light, trying to figure out what might be causing it. As he looked, the light in front of him coalesced, forming brilliant, glowing cherubim. The rest of the atmosphere around him continued to glow and shimmer, still coming from everywhere. But the cherubim just materialized out of coagulated light. They were ten feet tall, winged, with the countenance of a man, clothed in shimmery blue armor of light and carrying broadswords that radiated brilliant red light. Their piercing eyes twinkled with the starlight of a billion galaxies in deep dark pits.

Jason stood, jaw agape, mind reeling, trying to figure out what his eyes were beholding. All the questions that had swirled through his head just moments before were replaced with just one, "What the...?"

The cherubim angled their swords in such a way to challenge, but not threaten. A voice reverberated but exact origin unknown, "What do you seek?"

Swallowing hard, trying to pull his stomach out of his throat, Jason replied, "I'm looking for my nephew, Paulie."

The swords moved subtly, still not quite threatening, but more challenging than before. "What do you seek?" the cherubim asked again.

"My nephew, Paulie. He disappeared a few weeks ago. I thought maybe he came this way. Please, have you seen him?"

The cherubim quickly shifted their swords, clearly threatening now, light flashing everywhere, "What do you SEEK?"

Jason's mind whirled, thoughts clicked into place as he responded, "I go to seek a Great Perhaps!"

Prismatic light shot in all directions from the swords as the cherubim held them high above their heads. The snow stopped, the clouds cleared, and the prairie faded away into a beautiful garden, the cherubim standing as gate keepers at the entrance. A host of people in all manner of dress, as if from eras throughout history stood, smiling at Jason. At the front of the group, grinning from ear to ear, was Paulie. "Uncle Jason, I knew you'd figure out the clues to the Great Perhaps. Welcome to the Garden of Eden."

Remember the Ladies

Barbara Bartilson

Thirty years ago, Renee met Marie at a party for management trainees in the financial services industry. Marie made her living as a psychic medium and was part of the evening's entertainment.

Forever curious, Renee asked Marie, "So how do you know what you told the audience tonight?"

"Have you ever heard of the Akashic Record?"

Renee shook her head no.

Marie continued, "It is a record of everything that has ever happened. Some people can access it, some can't. For some reason, I have the ability."

"Is it something you can see or hear?"

"No, it's different than the five senses that most people have. It's hard to explain. Imagine you met someone who was totally blind since birth and you wanted to explain to them what colors are. How would you describe colors?"

"I see what you mean. That would be tough! So, is it in your mind like a thought?"

"You can try to put it into words, but I haven't found words that make sense to everybody. Some people have a hard time getting their heads around it."

"Is there something or somewhere I can read about the Akashic Record?"

"You might try the library, although it will take a while to research. It's hard to say where you may find insights. The Akashic Record is a storehouse of all information for every individual who has ever lived. Like a library of everything each of us has ever thought, felt, heard, seen, done, sensed, in all consciousness in all planes of realities. Scientists, philosophers, religious practitioners, psychics, writers and psychic healers reference it when needed. Those who access the Akashic Record perceive both the events and responses to those events based on past entries made throughout time. They consider past entries to determine potential future actions and probabilities. There is a thread of continuity through events from the beginning."

"From the beginning of time? How are events recorded?"

Renee had so many questions, but the party and the crowd pushed in on them.

Something about Marie's sincerity and maturity piqued Renee's curiosity. Renee began to consider that perhaps her interest stemmed from her college studies about the vocational rehabilitation of people with disabilities. She knew that the dilemma of how to describe colors to a blind person was real. Or perhaps it was simply that she always liked solving puzzles and problems, and discovering new paths and ideas. Maybe she was influenced by the odd experiences she had in college with the roommate she had called her Good Witch, or the experiences she had with her brother throughout life when unique events occurred at the same time to each of them, even when they were in completely different geographies.

Renee found herself daydreaming and imagining what it might be like to have this capability to access the Akashic Record. Any d?j? vu or occasional close encounter or weird happening made her wonder if maybe she had a small amount of psychic energy. How could she develop the ability? The conversation with the psychic Marie lingered in Renee's memory.

Then one day through an unexpected event at work she was convinced that she had some ability. A friendship with the CEO of a Fortune 500 grocery store chain began with a handshake at a business meeting. They both blushed when their hands touched. When he asked if they had met before, she offhandedly replied, "Not in this lifetime!" intending it to be a light, comical retort to save her from embarrassment. He asked if she had read *Many Lives, Many Masters* by Brian Weiss. She hadn't, so he announced that he would send the book to her and they must have coffee after she had read it. Their friendship sprouted and nourished her understanding of reincarnation and past life regression. They discovered a link to their blushing. This encounter gave Renee confidence and a thread of continuity back to Marie.

The note she had scribbled during her long ago visit for a private "reading" with Marie was still hidden in the top right drawer of her handmade dresser, next to the receipt for the Mikimoto pearls she had purchased with her first large bonus check. Putting on those precious pearls one morning, carefully handling the delicate thread that held them together, Renee saw the note and accepted the opportunity it presented. She vowed, "Today I will become an Akashic Record Keeper, or at least a chronicler of events!"

And so thirty years after Marie had entered her consciousness, Renee began to record events and responses. On January 25, 2017, she wrote,

There is a stone marker in Chicago's Hyde Park neighborhood, on the corner of East 53rd and South Dorchester, commemorating Michelle and Barack Obama's first date. I stopped abruptly on my first walk past the spot and looked around. The rock seemed out of place due to the small size, but there was something alive about it. The place is just a few blocks from their grand brick home off Hyde Park Avenue and near the proposed site of the new Presidential Library.

On this cold January morning as I hurried along 53rd Street, I was acutely aware of being in unfamiliar territory. Even after 20 years in this urban environment, I still find moments when I am

exhilarated to find new places and new things to do in this city that I have loved from the moment I arrived. I continued my walk to meet friends at the incubator site attached to the University of Chicago, excited to be doing some deep thinking and meaningful work after a dry spell.

When I walked back to my jeep, I stopped again at the stone marker, uncomfortable that I could not discern what I felt. Here in this burgeoning area with new small businesses, advanced students, and diverse faces, not far from neighborhoods of raw poverty and crime, the life forces of change swirled, a President had fallen in love and been nurtured here. What unknown forces collided to bring forth a leader of such strength, a leader who had the courage and privilege to change a nation into accepting a black President? Did it start here on this corner? Did the love he felt here on this corner have the power to sustain him through success and failure along his way? What about other Presidents? What forces had combined and interacted in their lives? Maybe I should investigate more First Ladies.

Renee began her research into first ladies with Abigail Adams. Somewhere she had read that Abigail was a strong-minded woman who had been critically important to her husband John's success as our nation's second President. As she watched the news on February 23, 2017, Renee thought about Abigail and wondered what she might have said to her husband if they still lived and were discussing today's news about the new President Trump. Renee opened her journal and wrote,

My Dearest John,

Thank goodness life continues after Earthly death. As I review the Akashic Record of our lives, I see our words are truly not lost. During our time on Earth in eighteenth century America, the hand-written, hand-carried paper letters we exchanged were the

only way to communicate over the vast distance that so often separated the Adams family. Unfortunately, time has disintegrated many of those original letters, and soon they will be lost to the ages. It is good the world can preserve the words in computers if not the tangible letters as evidence of the context. As you and I know, language changes meaning over time and generations. Do you know they still have over 1200 of our letters in the National Archives in Washington?

Remember our great gratitude for Mr. Gutenberg's 15th century printing press! Many books comforted us in our lonely and sad days apart. When I was most alone and worried about the children and money, I would reach for you through the books you recommended as if they could transport me to your side. You embraced me with the excitement of discussions you had with the like-minded gentlemen and even those whose interests conflicted with your own values. I read each night as if I could hold you in my bed.

Through our letters over many years we have continuously reflected on important topics including spousal battery, human bondage, and gender equality as the three issues I regret were not made right by the U.S. Constitutional Convention. I am pleased to have been privy to both your and Mr. Jefferson's heartfelt dilemmas and opinions on these issues, even though my plea for you to "Remember the Ladies" was not successful.

I beg your indulgence as I must continue the debate with you. A matter of great urgency has arisen here in recent time 21st century and we must find a way to change the political landscape lest those three matters be made worse and take us back to the days in this country of slaves, wives with no legal standing or protection from harm and injury, husbands with sovereign power over their spouse's body and activity, and girl children in every social class denied the chance to learn all things openly.

People throughout time have endeavored to improve communication through clear discourse and writing. However, people today are using devices to talk to each other in increasingly small doses. Even the current President in the United States of America has reduced his communication to a maximum of 140 characters per thought. His constituents debate how effective his words are, what his purpose is, and why he chooses this conveyance. People with the responsibility to act say they have no time to resolve the dilemma as they are unclear about the meaning of his messages. Some wonder that if he only has one thought of 140 characters per issue, can he possibly have seriously considered it? As generations before discovered, the people who think they know the one true answer, haven't yet understood the question. They believe they have no communication problem, when in fact, it is exactly all they have. t is currently under review whether this President has the mental real estate to house complete thoughts.

My dearest Friend, we must find a way to influence or return to Earth and contribute again to the diminishing well of understanding we gained in early America? What wisdom can we share from the lessons we learned as the nation was founded? How can we transfer those ideas from this place we now inhabit?

It seems people argue the same points and debate the same issues. Why do they not consider the fine works of Mr. Hamilton, Mr. Madison, and others? Are the Federalist and Anti-Federalist papers no longer available in the 21st century? Or is it just that people don't study history to learn lessons and transfer knowledge to new situations. We must find a way to communicate with them!!

Your Friend and Wife, Abigail

On March 15, 2017, after researching the ladies in Thomas Jefferson's life, Renee imagined that if people do have life after death, then the continuous thread to a next life might be devoted to improving conditions here on earth, influencing current events and corresponding with people of the past and with those still alive on earth. Mr. Jefferson's wife passed away before he was elected president and she made him promise not to remarry. Dolly Madison served him as a formal hostess at the White House. However, Sally Hemings, who was Mrs. Jefferson's half-sister, served him at home in his wife's stead until his death. Renee wrote words for Sally Hemings,

Dear Mrs. Adams,

Thank you for reaching out to me once again! I will be ready to re-incarnate when you send word! I look forward to another journey and I will begin contemplating the role I will play and the contribution I can make to our effort! will also confer with my half-sister, Mrs. Jefferson, and the lord of our Monticello, Mr. Thomas Jefferson, our master. The three of us are convinced we are bound through time and family to similar fates. I am certain they will want to contribute.

Abigail, you have been so very kind and instructive in allowing me to connect with you so easily. Only once was I able to reach Mr. Jefferson through quick-time, the e-Cloud. As in our life in the 18th century, his thoughts are generally occupied somewhere else, and not ready for my communication to him. I have frequently found this same trait in other men throughout my alternate, continuing life cycles. You are fortunate to have Mr. Adams with his constancy of purpose, direction, and ability to listen.

I have found that the problems between people are most often due to miscommunication, although if people are trying to communicate, I suppose we can have hope. I am very pleased with the increasing methods and tools available for communication. I just wish we all showed more civility for differing opinions.

I believe one of women's greatest contributions is our ability to effectively facilitate polite conversation; that ability born from women's desire to avoid the spousal battery and punishment allowed and protected under the law throughout time even in these United States. Women can smooth the way and hear the quiet in between words; they hear the tone, meaning, and the absence of meaning. Women understand what men so very rarely connect to the importance of an event. The men who do comprehend these important elements are often called leaders. Women are frequently diminished for the same qualities these men show.

Do you recall the contraption Mr. Jefferson built to copy his correspondence? He tied pens to opposite ends of a stick to capture an exact copy of what he was writing onto a second piece of paper. In today's world, e-printers connected to computers make the copies. Thomas told me that a copy allowed him to revisit his thoughts for deeper insight, consideration, and learning. Still today, he rarely sends communications quick-time through the e-Cloud due to his desire to more fully contemplate the impact of his messages and ponder the consequences.

His actions and moves take such a long time so he is not much fun at checkers or chess, but I suppose it is why he was perfect to draft the Declaration of Independence and the other great documents! He had an ability to combine and bring opposing points of view to a compromise without losing the support of the several sides. Oh, how I do wish someone like him existed today in the government of these United States. I agree with you, he needs to get back into today's political gambits!

Gaining alignment was a hard task in our last joint venture with only 13 states. I suppose we shouldn't be surprised at the difficulty in the 21st century considering there are now 50 states to bring to consensus. On top of that, there are the territories and so many other countries around the world to consider. Life today is akin to sitting on a powder keg about to explode. People might be happier if they were not so aware of what is going on all over the world. They know more, but have the same fears as people gone before.

I renewed my vows with Mr. and Mrs. Jefferson when we lived again in the 19ᵗʰ century. He and my sister and I have been striving to reverse what we believe may have been our misdeeds in the 15ᵗʰ century. We thought perhaps we could advance more quickly along the karmic timeline by working for the North's cause. I believe it helped to rid us of some of the evil we created long ago.

I am so very tired of trying to live down the trouble I fear I created for myself in the 15ᵗʰ century. Following an apprentice's path in my family's occupation was apparently not the best choice. I had benefit in the day, but as you know, I have paid for it ever since. I believe that is the great challenge my family has. Our past is the source of our karma. We are living out the lives we chose. When people take the easy road, they are destined to suffer the consequences in future lives. My family worked as executioners so I became one. My mother tried to convince me to take different work, but nothing else paid as well. There were plenty of beheadings. The condemned were charged a gratuity in advance to make sure we did it swiftly and with a sharp axe to avoid as much pain as possible. For so long now, we have been enslaved to pay back the price of the lives we took. If only it were easier to do the right things and enjoy the life we have. Money by ill-gotten gain always creates a life to be lived a-gain. Mr. and Mrs. Jefferson learned this as well. My family wants to move forward.

Like you, Abigail, I do believe Michelle has the qualities needed to be a political candidate! She is qualified and tempered for the challenge and ought to be a contender! Perhaps we should do all we can to blow the upcoming winds in her favor.

As ever,

Your Friend Sally Hemings

Renee finished her journal entries and pondered. People would never know of the events told here unless they could access the Akashic Record, as Renee did ... or until Renee wrote them down. Writing is the practice that gives her these glimpses into the Akashic Record. Curiosity continues to lead Renee on her writing journey, just as it led her to search for the answer to Marie's question of thirty years ago. How do you describe colors to a blind person?

1863, Redux

Gregory Wright

The two scientists met the visitors in the large conference room on the third floor of the administration building. Being casual, they sat in front of a large array of pastries and tall cups of coffee after brief introductions.

"What can we do for you today?" Cameron, the lead physicist asked. His compatriot, Steve Mendel, had a pad in front of him with an electric pencil ready to take notes.

"Well Cameron," began Jonathan Alder, one of the visitors, "my colleague here, Dr. Ginsburg, has an intriguing offer for your agency."

Steve and Cameron exchanged looks. "What would two political scientists want with our department?"

"Currently, as you both well know, we are in a political situation where extreme views are dictating centrist policy. This isn't an uncommon situation, in fact, we now call them Great Regressions, in which government and society become unstable and reactionary." Dr. Alder glanced over at Dr. Ginsburg as if handing the baton to the next runner.

"We are familiar with your work in time travel and have read a number of your papers on historical retrieval and documentation." Dr. Ginsburg continued, running his fingers nervously through his thick red hair.

There was a pause as the two political scientists prepared the pitch. "We would like to use your machine to arrive at a time where we can draw information that would be useful in reminding people of our need to bolster our democracy rather than pull it apart."

Steve interjected with the forcefulness of an ultimatum, "You realize that whomever we send, we cannot bring back."

Drs. Ginsburg and Alder both nodded.

"You also realize that we cannot have anyone there alive longer than 24 hours. In essence, it is a death sentence, which is why we only offer this opportunity to specific individuals." Steve mentioned with equal intensity.

Dr. Ginsburg lowered his head and folded his hands in his lap. "I have just been diagnosed with terminal cancer. I have already received my death sentence. Therefore, I will be the one going."

There was a pause among the four as Steve and Cameron digested the information.

"I believe that satisfies your criteria?" Dr. Alder added.

"It does." Cameron said softly.

"I understand the parameters." Dr. Ginsburg began. "But given the extreme political situation we have, we feel this is our opportunity to add visual documentation to defuse a dire political stalemate."

"Do you have a specific time and place?"

"Yes." Dr. Ginsburg stated.

"This is an amazing sacrifice." Steve said. "At this point, unless Cameron has any objections, I feel this is an option we can explore."

Cameron nodded in agreement.

"Well then," Steve continued, " we will need you to be fitted for the correct uniform along with a few other cosmetic features. We will be in touch."

With all four of them accepting the agreement, Dr. Ginsburg reached over and grabbed his third Danish. "I'm going to miss these."

The two scientists, focused by the intensity of their mission, left the airport in the rented car, following the exits out of Baltimore to head toward their destination in the Pennsylvania countryside. They had flown in from Texas and were unaccustomed to the early autumn fall chill. In preparation, however, they had their outdoor gear ready. Their tanned faces were at odds with the dark colors of the winter coats. They said little as they began the three-hour drive, the silence driven more by their goal than any lack of friendship.

About an hour and a half later, they pulled over to stretch their legs and get something to eat. At a roadside diner, they found a clean booth, far away from the cold draft of the doors, and ordered simple hamburgers and fries.

"So, do you think it's there?'

Cameron shrugged. "The cemetery is there, so why wouldn't it be?"

"Still amazes me that we can launch a man into the past, and we can leave immediately to retrieve him within a few hours.

"The whole idea of time travel is unique. Lucky we haven't blown ourselves up yet. What seems sobering to me is that one of our subjects could have changed history, and we would never know."

Steve shrugged in agreement. "I could have been a model 30 seconds ago."

Cameron smiled at the joke, "I don't think so Steve, you're not capable in any dimension."

Steve smiled. "Come on Cameron, it could happen." And they both chuckled at the image and the absurdity.

They finished their meal and resumed the last leg of their journey. When they were within a half an hour, Steve reached into the back seat and pulled a small monitoring device out of the side of his satchel. "Hope we can find him today. I don't like staying away from home any more than I have to."

"I hear ya."

Playing with some toggles, he tested the battery and the range. Convinced all was operative, he set the monitor down on his lap and stared blankly out the window as the car reached the Gettysburg city limits.

Driving slowly through the farms and then into the downtown, Cameron ignored the signs directing people to the battlefield and instead looked for the subtle signage directing them to Evergreen Cemetery.

Reaching the tall limestone pillars, they stopped by the entrance and checked in at the office. Waiting for them was a sheriff's deputy, the proprietor of the cemetery and two gravediggers lounging by the coffee machine in the front reception area.

They entered, passed through the reception office, as the deputy nodded to the two grave diggers and followed the two other gentlemen to a back office where they closed the door.

The deputy spoke first. "So you are the guys from a lab?" The deputy asked.

"I am Steve Mendal and this is Cameron Daely. We are from the Time Distribution and Reclamation Office."

The officer and cemetery executive looked at each other with a blank expression, not sure what to say.

"We are a research section of a government bureau that retrieves information on important historical events." Cameron chimed in.

For some reason the recognition of the word 'research' made the two local men relax.

"Well, here is the dig order from the judge." the officer said, pulling a tri-fold piece of paper from his back pocket. I need to go with you of course, but it seems pretty simple."

The scientists nodded in agreement. Steve took the paper and slipped it into an interior pocket of his coat.

They all left the small room, the executive returned to his desk while the two scientists and the deputy exited the building with the two gravediggers falling in behind them. Outside, the scientists returned to their car, one of the workers sliding into the back seat to act as the guide, with the other worker and the deputy following in the cemetery's pickup.

Under the digger's direction, they proceeded to a plot far in the back of the cemetery. "If he's anywhere, he would be here," the digger reasoned. When they reached a section set aside for veterans that had died after the battle, they pulled to the side of the gravel road. Leaving the vehicles clustered in a group, Steve took out the monitor he was working on and held it level in front of him. It was square, one foot on either side with a radar screen in the center and a panel with a few toggles on the side. Simple.

"Here we go." The machine began to hum softly as Steve watched the screen's lighted waves of sonar echo over the landscape. The men made themselves comfortable on the tailgate of the truck, while the deputy leaned against the car and did business on his iphone. Steve began to walk in a straight line, slowly following a grid pattern on the monitor. Cameron trailed at first, but lost interest as Steve began a third pass as directed by the sonars grid.

After about an hour and a half, he had completed almost two thirds of the plot when a chime began sounding, catching everyone's attention. The deputy straightened up, the workers jumped off the truck to grab their shovels, and Cameron rose from the backseat of the car. Quickly searching a satchel on the ground next to him, Steve pulled out another small handheld monitor - eight inches square. Composed of a screen, with small function buttons located on the sides.

"Got it." Steve said, stating the obvious. Turning a few degrees in either direction, he then locked down the location and walked 15 feet towards the east, the chime now becoming more frequent until it slipped into a solid tone. Looking up, Steve saw he was standing in front of a grave marked UNKNOWN, Nov. 1863.

"The date works." He said. "This must be it."

His search completed, he stepped aside as the two gravediggers began their work. Digging was a task they did every day, so they were quickly down about three feet when one of the shovels hit something wooden with a dull thud. Scraping now instead of digging, they uncovered the lid to a simple pine coffin. In an effort to speed the process, without a directive the deputy went back to the truck and returned with a crowbar and small sledge hammer. He handed them to the men in the hole and the lead digger slipped it under the grey wood. With a few solid strokes, the lid loosened and the two men reached into the gap to pull the lid upward.

They stood silently staring at the thin skeleton laid out in front of them. Dressed in the faded blue uniform of a Union cavalry officer, the body was askew, the head slightly tilted to one side. The coffin had held together amazing well. The body was intact, although awkwardly placed as it must have shifted when interred. Caught up in the drama of it all, they stood silently around the hole. The gravediggers, climbing out of the shallow grave, wiped their hands on their coveralls and slid the blades of their shovels into the piles of soil to wait as the scientists finished their work.

Steve and Cameron slid into the grave with clumsy effort, trying hard not to fall on the skeleton. Cameron had the screen out, ready for the process, while Steve took a few minutes to stare at the skull, the jaw opened slightly, the red puffs of hair in a cluster underneath a cavalryman's hat.

"Hard to believe he was alive this morning."

The deputy was now confused. "That's an odd thing to say." He said.

"Not really," Cameron said. "You see, he was sent back in time to gather information for us. He knew there was no way back, so it was essentially a suicide mission."

"But couldn't he change history? Asked the deputy.

"No," Steve said, "he had a delayed cyanide capsule injected into his bloodstream allowing only 24 hours to live once he was transferred. Our concern was that he couldn't complete his mission or if he did, where the body would be buried."

"By setting him up as a veteran, we knew he would be interred in this part of the cemetery when he died." Cameron said.

"What mission was that?" one of the gravediggers asked.

"Hopefully, you will soon see." Steve said, and he leaned over the man's chest and dusted away some of the dried fabric from his tunic. Exposing a brass button at the top of the uniform, Steve slipped a set of small scissors from his pocket, cut away the thread holding it, and passed the button to Cameron. Cameron then took the button and slipped it into a small slot in the back of the smaller machine.

"You see, that button actually holds a camera. Everything he saw was recorded."

Cameron held the monitor out at arm's length so they could all see. From the back of the truck, the two gravediggers climbed into the bed to see over the scientist's shoulder. When Steve climbed out of the grave, the deputy stood next to him leaning over in amazement at the screen in front of them. All of them silently watched for a video as Cameron turned on the unit, and waited patiently as he sifted through the files, searching for the appropriate drive.

Suddenly the screen cleared and there was a slow motion to the camera as the soldier walked out of the woods where he was teleported, and through farm fields and over a narrow dirt road towards a large collection of people by an open field. A crowd that was getting larger by the minute.

"Testing audio." the soldier said as he moved closer into the crowd and tried to advance towards the stage where a lecturer was just finishing. In the distance, they could hear a hymn being sung. The scientists and their audience were silent as they stared at the video of life two hundred years before. A snapshot of life was like back then. Reaching the stage just in time, the subject stood there, the button camera recording the shuffling of the presenters, the awkwardness of the soldiers guarding the stage and the sudden appearance of a tall bearded man in a long black suit. Two sheets of paper were clutched in his hands.

Speaking in a surprisingly high, almost reedy voice, he began; "Four score and seven years ago....".

The small audience watched raptured as the first video of the Gettysburg Address was played out to them. When it had been completed, they stood there quietly, the deputy looking from the video to the grave and back again.

"Mission accomplished." Steve said, breaking the silence.

"We have it for the ages." Cameron said.

"What happens now?" one of the diggers asked softly.

"We post it so everyone can see it, just as this mission was intended to do." Steve said. "This is something we can all get inspiration from, that at the most pivotal moment is U.S. history, a statement such as this inspired hope in the future. Everyone should be able to share in this and realize we are going to be okay if we are united. It's not just words anymore. Now the video can speak."

As Steve was speaking, they could hear Dr. Ginsburg on the video as he was walking away from the crowd. "Feeling weak and mouth is dry." He said thickly. "Poison seems to be kicking in early. I am posting this note on my uniform as requested. He held out a small slip of paper in front of the button, difficult to read as he walked, but for a second it was legible. 'Bury me with my friends' was all it said. After a few, moments, they heard the soldier say he was pinning it to his uniform and that he was heading to a copse of trees not far away.

Once the screen went blue, Cameron moved the files, and then sent the video. Once completed, he snapped the tunic button out of it's slot and put it in the breast pocket of his shirt.

Looking down at the body once more, he solemnly declared "Gentlemen, please rebury Doctor Ginsburg. He was a true patriot." The deputy nodded to them as if giving official permission.

The gravediggers jumped back in the hole and carefully replaced the lid of the coffin, hammering the lid back into place with a supply of fresh nails in their pockets.

Steve and Cameron shut down their machines, softly discussed a few facts between themselves and began the walk to the car.

"So where are you off to now?" the deputy asked.

Steve said over his shoulder, "Philadelphia."

Once More, With Feeling

Tanasha Martin

All exhilaration fades.

The curl of my lips falters. My stomach plummets. Pieces of me break? Disappear?

Disintegrate.

Fillings vibrate, regress to powder and a metallic taste coats my tongue and the edge of my throat. Pins in my right elbow from a ice skating accident in the eighth grade shrink, leaving my arm to dangle at my side. Then—it heals.

Sweet God, no.

The return disc.

I pinch the inside of my left wrist as if I could hold it in place. The components contract beneath my skin and become microscopic bits that absorb into my bloodstream.

My lids close. Instruments play in my mind. Woodwinds and percussion soothe, wave after wave, until high strings take over the melody and meld into rational thought and observations.

Concentrate.

1. Foreign objects in the body are destroyed upon arrival to this time.

The Gossamer Bridge Grant was my symphony. The experiment of the century, bound to make the biggest mark on human history. Movement through time. A flight as tenuous as a fly through a spider's funnel web.

2. Sound: the first sense activated.

Light, unfamiliar classical music actually plays. It chimes like bells and flows like water. This time appears from murky, swirling ether to crystal clear, hard edges.
In success is failure. I've made it here.
But, my silken thread home—snipped.

To rematerialize is a risky proposition. Travel to the past is safer. There is security in knowing the building walls, columns, streets and likely space occupied by people. *What is the challenge in that?*
The future is unmapped and unrecorded. The pinnacle of achievement. Or should be.
So, appearance in front of, instead of inside of another person—not so bad.

3. Time displacement successful. Same space. Lab seems reasonably changed.

4. No "landing." Travel takes...17.5 seconds.

5. No pain. Internal metal and electronic material was replaced by... organic material?

6. Heartbeat heightened, but normal.

7. Air is clean and breathable.

8. Inhabitants: Human.

9. First contact: Female.

The blinking woman doesn't move or speak. Her straight black hair covers the name tag on her lab coat. The coffee in her cup ripples between her hands.

I force a gentle smile. My dark tone of skin may be an issue in this time—especially with so much of it on display. *Ease her discomfort.* I touch one hand to the sparse hair on my chest. My words are soft—mezzo-piano in a cavernous room. "Dr. Vernon Gaul. You are?"

She snaps out of her trance and sets her cup on the tabletop beside her. She swallows, slips from her white coat, and extends her hand. "Dr. Nasima Shir. Cold?"

I accept the coat and as I slip it on, grip her hand. "Dr. Shir, a pleasure. I'm conducting an experiment: time displacement. May I ask the year?"

She tilts her head, focused. "Twenty sixty-seven." Her smile is resplendent and her voice is stronger. "As perfect a time as you will ever find. No illness, no crime, every soul is satisfied. Even our arts are computer-generated perfection."

Thrill and dread are wings that beat against the same edge of this time. The music overhead feels discordant, but isn't.

10. Neither my name nor work are recognized.

I sleep on a sofa in the lab and spend months in research with Dr. Shir. She sets her own research aside like used gum and flurries about, eager to demonstrate the superiority of her utopian time. She expresses a desire to visit the past—purely as validation.

352. Technology equivalent to initial experiment does not exist here. Old technology is discarded. It cannot adequately be reproduced.

I rub my forehead. This time, the swell of music that lingers in my mind is faint. A saxophone lilting a tune of bittersweet dreams. A song my mother would play whenever a bad day had dampened her spirits. She'd say, "It gives me comfort to know others have gone through hard times and still manage to share something beautiful with the world."

But hope dissolves when there is nothing to feed it.

I stretch and determine that time isn't going to displace itself. I brace for the push-back. "Nasima, could you find some music from my time?"

Her voice is familiar static. "Why? This piece is beautiful. It's perfect in every way. No wrong chords, no missed notes, no timing mishaps. The best there is to offer!"

Don't let the request drop this time.

My eyes sting and my voice is thick. "Please? Familiarity may spark creativity."

She's right. One flawless song after another. But I crave a break in a singer's voice. Mood. Tone. An invisible tether to the soul of another. A common toil, mutually understood turmoil, a lost dream. That elusive agonizing swell in the music. The harried scrawl of a lyric in tune with the voice of humankind.

Frisson. Emotion. Unappreciated, until they are gone.

Nasima swivels her chair to the interactive glass over the meeting table. The computer authorizes her through voice print and pulls up the archived data. She rises and with a stiff hand, gestures toward the screen. The click of heels on cool tile echo her retreat.

The next few hours are filled with a web of melodies. I cocoon myself and emerge whole. No longer the fly, but the spider. Glide on the silk. Rework my web. From funnel to orb. These materials will work if I build my bridge on a different design.

431. Advancement lies not only in what we gain, but also retaining what we have.

In failure is success.

Now: *Once more, with feeling.*

Handwavium

Todd Hogan

Handwavium[1]

A Fantasy with Footnotes

By

Todd Hogan[2]

"Follow me," Gertrude's ICPA[3] supervisor said when she arrived at work.

Her supervisor led her to the conference room. When Gertrude saw the stone-faced guards nicknamed the Four Horsemen of the Apocalypse (4HotA) positioned outside the room, she knew who was waiting for her.

"Hello, Dad."

"My angel. No kiss for your father? That's better. Sit, sit."

Gertrude was twenty-nine years old, but she always felt like a pre-teen around her father. He had aged, though. There was more gray in his hair. He kept his glasses on longer. He stooped a little. But whenever she

---

[1] Early philosophers believed that a powerful substance existed that could change an impossible event into one that was entirely probable, if not inevitable. Like Einstein's General Theory of Relativity, electromagnetic waves, and the Higgs Boson "God" particle, the mathematical proof for the existence of handwavium (HW) preceded man's ability to produce it consistently.

[2] Pseudonym — Author's name concealed for her personal protection.

[3] International Chronological Protection Agency, an organization established to keep all the world's clocks synchronized. Secretly, however, the ICPA works insidiously to combat the unfettered use of handwavium.

smelled the fine cigars he had just extinguished, felt his gentle touch on her shoulder, and saw the expensive cut of his bespoke suit, she recognized his authority over her.

"What's this I hear?" he said, as softly as his blunt manner permitted. She heard the slight gravel in his throat. "You and some egg-head?"

She knew who he meant, though she had tried to be discrete.

"Niels is a Senior Fellow at the Handwavium Institute[4]," she said. "That's better than winning a MacArthur Fellowship. Please don't judge, or mess this up for me, Dad."

Her father's heavy fingers drummed the tabletop.

"You know we don't allow fraternization between scientists and ICPA members, right?"

"But he's Niels Borger[5]!" Gertrude couldn't control a smile so buried her face in her hands.

"I can't bend the rules, not even for my daughter. Besides, what do you really know about this guy?"

"Niels invented the handwavium light wave detector[6]. He eliminated

---

[4]Warring nations scrambled to discover a reliable source of HW. The United States began its Manhattan Project to develop nuclear weapons. But an even more secret aspect of the Project was to develop HW. Contemporaneously with nuclear fission, the US found the nearly mythical process to produce handwavium, and the Handwavium Institute was begun. The relative moral weight of these discoveries can be measured by one fact — President Truman dropped the atomic bomb twice, but used HW only once. In 1948, Truman used HW to win the presidential election where Thomas Dewey was so favored to win that the newspaper headlines had already been printed.

[5]Niels Borger, Senior Fellow at the Handwavium Institute and one of the few who was still single after working there longer than seven years. He had been recruited by the Institute upon completion of his PhD in probability and electromagnetic radiation. Niels had no idea the Handwavium Institute even existed. He thought their generous offer was an April Fool's prank, until he read their non-disclosure agreements, their non-compete clauses, and the penalties for violation of the Government Secrets Act. He laughed; the woman making his offer didn't.

[6]Discovering Handwavium is even more difficult than finding enriched uranium. Handwavium radiates light waves at frequencies that are usually undetectable. ICPA investigating the improbable popularity of disco music noticed the proliferation of disco balls and pulsating lights, which were used to mask the large quantities of HW lightwaves emitted. When these waves hit any prismatic structure (such as condensation on a shot glass), they split into an intense, visible rainbow spectrum. At dance clubs, the HW rainbows

so much of the guesswork in policing the improper use[7] of HW. He's the reason we locate HW with as much accuracy as a Geiger counter detects uranium."

Her father shook his head sadly. "He's given notice. He wants to exit the Handwavium Institute."

An involuntary shudder passed through Gertrude. She remembered what had happened to Werner Heisenbill, whose body was never found.

"No!" she said, jumping to her feet so she was taller than her father. "Niels doesn't mean it. He only wants a vacation. He likes to visit time travel sites around the world."

"That's the problem. Time travel is never allowed. Ever!" He smacked the table with his fist.

"He won't violate the time travel paradox[8]!"

"No one leaves the Institute." said her father with a note of finality.

"Can't you make an exception[9]?" Her hands were clasped tightly.

Her father solemnly shook his head.[10]

---

were indistinguishable from the other "light-noise" broadcast. Once discovered, bans were imposed on the unlimited use of pulsing lights, lasers and flash-bangs, and the disco music craze collapsed like an overstretched helium balloon.

[7] In response to the danger posed by the misuse of HW, the International Chronological Protection Agency was established. Its members were supplied by the global gaming industry, from Vegas to Monte Carlo. They were ruthless in prohibiting unauthorized use of HW, especially in economic instances.

[8] The danger of time travel consists of well-documented paradoxes. Was it possible to go back in time to kill your own grandfather or marry your own grandmother? Could you ground all flights on 9/11? Could you change the course of history by assassinating Hitler? The last scenario might mean that there was no World War II, that the Manhattan Project never occurred, and that handwavium had not been discovered. Thus, the paradox.

[9] The ICPA sometimes overlooked the incidental use of HW in championship contests, which made the outcome unpredictable and kept the games interesting. After all, the viewing public loved to see long-shot come-from-behind victories like Super Bowl LI. Occasionally, HW provided the music industry with an improbable hit song, usually a single hit for the performer.

[10] As wildly unlikely events occurred globally, concerned scientists, economists and casino operators took note. The casino operators who had benefitted from HW when they opened operations in the middle of a desert, watched Las Vegas improbably grow to become the destination playground of many adults. But their overwhelming concern was that HW might be used to skew the odds in favor of a particular gambler to the detriment of the house. Such a situation could spell financial disaster for the casinos. The

"How much time until...?" She couldn't finish her question.

"He's given thirty days' notice, but termination occurs on a day of our choosing, at midnight."

"I have to say good-bye." Tears formed and Gertrude immediately wiped them away.

"Angel, don't torture yourself. I can set you up with any number of trusted men if you like."

She shook a slim finger at him. "Not Two-fingers Feeney. Not Cottonmouth. Not your four horsemen outside. Do you know me at all?"

"You're my angel, my little girl. Nothing less than a consigliere for you."

"Forget it!"

Gertrude turned on her heel, and ran to the door. She didn't slam it, but closed it very firmly. The 4HotA didn't change their stone faces, but she was offended by the devilment in their eyes.

She hurried to Niels's lab and burst in. Niels looked up, wearing night vision goggles with oversized eyepieces. With his long, thin frame, he looked like an insect, but a sweet one.

Gertrude hugged him, pinning his arms.

"You can't leave," she said. "Nobody leaves the Handwavium Institute."

"Hello, Gertrude." Niels wiggled free and took off his headgear. "Of course people leave. Remember Werner Heisenbill? The one who won the lottery five years ago? He's off enjoying his money."

Gertrude sniffed back tears.

"No, Niels, he isn't. Werner disappeared *because* he won the lottery. Nobody from the Institute is allowed to gamble. When Werner won, it raised red flags."

"Lotteries are supposed to be improbable."

"Exactly. He couldn't prove it was a random fluke that he won, and so he was 'disappeared'." She made air quotes. "Nobody leaves here. It's like working with Blood Diamonds. I can't stand to lose you."

Gertrude held him close again until Niels began to blush and squirm.

ICPA ruthlessly enforced control of HW.

"Is that why you gave me those HW-doctored apples?" he asked. "They put me in mind of my grandfather's orchard."

"I used such a little bit. I wanted to surprise you."

"I knew you were using HW on me, but I liked remembering those times."

His notebooks lined several shelves. The most recent apples she had given him rested on a laboratory sheet in front of his HW detector and a picture of his family's orchard.

"How did you know?" she asked.

Niels patted the head gear. "This baby," he said. "It's an improved HW detector, built especially for the more powerful HW illusions generated these days[11]."

"New, more powerful HW?"

"It really affects perception. If the target is suggestible, then he sees or hears what the supplier wants, not what's really there. Almost assuredly, it was used in the last three presidential campaigns[12]."

"And those goggles help the viewer to see reality?"

Niels grinned sheepishly. "Well, who's to say what reality is..."

Gertrude pointed at the notebooks on the shelf. "Is this everything about your new discovery?"

"I have notes on the computer, too, but for the most part, this is it."

"Okay," she said. "I have an idea that just might save you."

"Save me from what?" he asked.

Gertrude patted his cheek. "From yourself. I'll meet you at your condo tonight at 8:00."

---

[11] Many historians believe HW was used to help elect JFK in 1960 and Bill Clinton in 1992.

[12] Conservatives probably used it to elect Bush over Gore, and Trump over Hillary Clinton. Even more disturbing are the implications of the Hillary Clinton loss: Bill Clinton had access to HW, and yet Hillary lost two elections; therefore, an even stronger HW was available to Barack Obama and to Donald Trump that overcame the HW that Bill Clinton had used. The difference was as great as the gap between the atomic and the hydrogen bombs. Like nuclear proliferation, this evolution was inevitable but could send us back to the stone age.

Niels frowned. "I have to work. Sorry."

Gertrude loved his work ethic, but he didn't understand the danger. There was one thing that would ensure his rendezvous.

"Have you seen "Somewhere in Time"?[13]" she asked.

His eyes lit up. "It's used to be my favorite movie! Christopher Reeve and Jane Seymour! But, Fellows at the Institute agree to forego viewing time travel movies. It's a condition of employment."

"Don't worry; I'll get a copy. I'll smuggle it tonight to your place. But, if this is going to work, you'll have to leave your professional life here."

"What life? I live for vacations. Why do you think I'm leaving?"

"When you leave tonight, take only what's important to you. We're not coming back, okay?"

"We?"

"Oh, and you need to destroy all your notes and those headgear prototypes."

"Three years of my life?"

"Otherwise, it will be the end of your life, and mine, too. Trust me?"

Niels studied her like the detail plate from a particle accelerator — closely, intensely, and dispassionately. Gertrude felt uncomfortable at first, until she realized that he was the first man to have looked at her so closely. Her father frowned on that kind of red-blooded scrutiny of his angel. She enjoyed the attention, and smiled.

"Okay," he said. "I'm with you."

At 8:00 that night, Gertrude showed up at Niels's condo. He had empty research boxes but had kept the two headgear prototypes. She brought a container of HW, some apples, and a blu-ray of "Somewhere in Time". They savored the movie together, and Niels cried. Periodically, she looked out his front window, and saw that her father had sicced his 4HotA on Niels.

"Tonight?" she worried. It was only 30 minutes to midnight.

---

[13] Lovers separated by decades improbably meet at the Grand Hotel on Mackinac Island, music by John Williams who uses a Rachmaninoff rhapsody on a theme by Pagnini.

"Are you ready to start your new life?" she asked. She pulled out the container with enough HW to last a lifetime.

Niels was shocked. "What are you thinking?" he said. "It's bad enough that you talked me into rewatching the movie. But this?" He pointed to the container on his table.

"With HW, we can watch time travel films whenever we want. Are you ready?"

Niels bit his lip. "I don't know."

Gertrude felt like shaking him, then realized the fault might be hers, not his.

"Look," she said. "I get it. Institute Fellows are all married to the most beautiful people. They may not be able to gamble, but the ICPA allows all Fellows to use just enough HW to marry models, rock stars and movie stars. I know I'm no Cable News Anchor, but..."

"It's not that," Niels said. "I think you're lovely and thoughtful and kind of scary. But I was thinking of my prototypes. I don't think I can let the world go on when certain people have the power to distort reality. This headgear helps them see the world and its leaders the way they truly are."

Gertrude took his hands and held them until he looked into her eyes. She was impressed by the naive decency of this man. It would be a shame if he lost his life at so young an age.

"Niels," she said, "you give the world too much credit. People can always see the truth if they pay attention. But they don't want to see the cold hard facts. They want the fantasy. They want stories, fables, movies, and songs. They would rather fight vampires and zombies than injustice and prejudice. You might give everyone the ability to see the real problems, but nobody, NOBODY, would thank you for it."

Niels shook his head. "So, that's the kind of world we're going to live in?"

Gertrude nodded. "Emphasis on 'going to live.'" She lightly dusted four apples. "For my friends downstairs. I'll be right back."

Niels softly kissed her cheek. Gertrude kissed him back on the lips, then left with four apples.

The 4HotA traded snide smiles when they saw her. "It's smart you're leaving. Saves us some trouble."

Gertrude offered them the apples. "You'll need your strength." She watched as each man took at least a small bite.

"That guy is so boring," she told them. "The entire building is full of old people."

They nodded in thoughtful agreement, without noticing that she slipped back into the condo building.

When Gertrude returned to Niels, two headgear were on the table. He said, "We should keep these for our protection."

She was beginning to think he was hopeless. It was nearly midnight.

They stood in the living room, each saying goodbye to the world they knew. Gertrude looked out his front window to check on her father's men. The 4HotA were on alert, apples cores tossed aside. One man checked his watch. Another looked up and saw her in the window. He nodded to her and then spoke an order to the others. They started into the building.

"They're coming," she said. "Remember our movie." She kissed him again, and took out a generous spoonful of HW for their own use. Then under one headgear, she placed a small card. It said, "For Dad, with Love. You can see me as I truly am."

The HW worked its magic. She took the arm of the man Niels had become, and he happily walked out with her. They passed the 4HotA in the lobby, waiting for an up elevator. One of them said, "Ain't you got no manners? Make room for the nice older couple, guys."

Gertrude was confident then that the 4HotA perceived a shuffling elderly couple. But she knew Niels saw Jane Seymour holding his arm, and she saw Christopher Reeve, ready to start their lovely new lives in a world limited only by their imaginations.

Otherness

Tim Yao

A poem about our possible near future

Heartless others thought of me no doubt
Self-serving and filled with greed
Even I cringe now at who I was.

Poisoned by talk shows blaring with bias
I watched the faux news
Avoided truth, closed my eyes.

The poor were undeserving after all
They were lazy, different, not like me.
I shied away from learning
    how they were imprisoned in their suffering.

More than that, I thought it okay
To support the policies of wealth
Lowering taxes and increasing profits.

Then one day a friend shared a game, a virtual game
Unlike any I had played before

An immersive experience.

I played the role no I lived it
Her story compelling
Heartbreaking.

Jandi was a teenaged girl
Living on the streets
Homeless through no fault of her own.

She worked hard every day
To help her young siblings
Studied in school when she could.

Virtual reality through my headset
Pricey enough to have housed Jandi
And her family for months.

Every in-game decision I made to help her
Showed the futility
Trapped as she was by her circumstance.

Every sad act and indignity Jandi suffered
Haunted my dreams
I could not sleep when I learned her story to be true.

Truth begets truth.
Light blazed in my darkness.
We must act when we feel the hurts of others.

I followed the link the game provided,
met Jandi and her family.

My outside help opens opportunities to them,
   starting with a home.

Those who made this game
gave each player a different, real person to follow.
Artificial intelligence makes this possible.

New empathy has changed me forever,
made me more comfortable in my skin.
Once your eyes are open, you must look and act.

I now pursue social justice,
help to spread the word,
because they helped me walk a mile in her shoes.

The Lightning Chamber

Elaine Fisher

The sun shone down onto the kitchen sink piled high with a week's worth of dirty dishes. Madison struggled to maneuver his rolling walker over to the counter. He turned on the NOAA - All Hazard Weather Radio that his son bought for him.

"For the Miami Beach area... partly cloudy, hot, and humid with a high of 90 degrees, thunderstorms in the evening, chance of rain 80 percent..."

Throughout his life, he felt more at home with machines than with people. No one could believe he was able to find someone as warm and understanding as his wife, Angie. Through their years together, for all of his brilliance as a scientist and inventor, he was not wise in the matters of the heart. Until Angie died, then his heart painfully came alive.

The weather radio continued to replay the forecast, filling the kitchen with cold scientific chatter until it finally got Madison's attention.

"Thunderstorms in the evening... chance of rain... Hey, Buddy, are you even listening to me?"

Madison swore at the radio while smacking its glowing blue bar until it stopped its repeating.

What was happening to him? He never heard voices before, and they were happening more frequently. Only yesterday, he had an argument with a bird that landed on his kitchen windowsill, squawking at him for making excuses for staying inside.

171

Oh God, why would he answer these voices as if they were real?

One time, he asked Angie if she thought he was mad; she laughed with a soft bird-like trill. Her laughter was natural and melodic, whereas his erratic laughter and behavior struck most people as odd and eccentric. Only Angie knew what to say to him.

"Madie, my love, you're not mad; they just don't understand you. They do not have the ability to look beyond your voice, beyond your behavior. And it doesn't help that your hair is always wild, especially after being out in a rainstorm."

Madison reached up almost expecting to feel Angie's hand smoothing out his long curly hair.

Her soothing voice continued in his mind.

"If only you could let the storm heal you, the lightning can spark those feelings buried deep in you. Brighten up your eyes, the windows to your soul."

Through the years, his rational, scientific mind had always refuted her spiritual beliefs. He only paid attention to what made sense to him, tuning out the rest.

It seemed like all of the bad things that could happen to him came at once. His wife died only two months ago after a long illness. The last few days of her life, he hid himself away, not going into their bedroom that had become the 'death chamber' to him. He sprained his ankle, the day before the funeral resulting in his decision not to attend. It was a terrible excuse, but her death filled him with such unexplainable loss and despair. He buried his head in his old research papers, anything to distract him from his uncomfortable feelings. The day after the funeral, he broke his other leg. Nick, his son, said it was a deserved punishment. Their already shaky relationship became even more troubled.

Madison swallowed the pain medicine his son dutifully brought him. He found no good reason to move about so he spent most of his time sitting and sleeping in the La-Z-Boy chair in the living room. In his mind, the bedroom had become a 'sacred chamber,' the closed door like a guardian warding off strangers.

Madison ate only when he was hungry, which was not often. Nick would bring him groceries and other necessities. The infrequent and short visits suited Madison fine, who did not like his son's criticism on how he lived his life. Ironically, they shared a common interest — weather, especially lightning and thunder. Florida had the highest amounts of lightning strikes in the nation and his son was a meteorologist in Miami.

Madison rolled back the wrinkled sleeves of his unwashed shirt and sank his hands deep into the water, scrubbing at the crusty and greasy plates with a soapy rag. His son would be coming this evening. A sink full of dishes would not be an acceptable sight and he wanted to avoid any confrontations.

He wrung out the rag, closed his eyes, and tried to visualize his wife, the peacemaker in the family. Instead, the angry face of Nick appeared for a brief moment, then the image violently whirled down the drain and was gone.

Out the kitchen window, birds scattered through the sky, squawking their warning of the upcoming storms.

The rain pelted his windshield as Nick pulled into the parking lot of his father's apartment building. He climbed out of his car, pulled out his umbrella, stepped into a deep puddle, and swore aloud as he ran for the entrance. As he swung open the door, a bright flash of light and a crash of thunder encouraged him in.

Thunder always brought memories of his mother who had often tried to cover up the sound with her own laughter. She had a lovely sense of humor, in contrast to his father whose rare, strange laughter would come at such inappropriate times.

In the foyer, he pushed the button marked Madison Wexler and waited for the buzzer. The locked door clicked and he yanked it open. Having no patience to wait for the elevator, he stomped up three flights of stairs and down the long corridor to his father's apartment.

He reached the apartment exhausted and agitated. Taking a few calming breaths, he finally knocked, and then impatiently rang the bell. The door slowly opened. His father blankly stared at him. At one time, he had despised his father's cold, piercing, blue eyes, but at least they were more alive than the double pools of dead calm water that were looking at him now.

"Can I come in?" Nick finally asked.

Madison nodded, backed up, and turned his rolling walker, leading him into the living room. He shuffled to his La-Z-Boy chair and reclined in it.

At the persisting silence, Nick defensively asked, "Are you mad at me, Dad? I offered to take you out for dinner, but you said not to bother, you had already taken something out."

"Not mad. Had a fine dinner...can take care of myself."

"Alright." Nick turned away glancing at the messy apartment, a stack of unread newspapers sat by the La-Z-Boy. He walked into the kitchen and put away the groceries he had bought.

At the steady sound of rumbling thunder, he came back to the living room. Once more, he thought of his mother's laughter, sad that he would never hear it again.

The constant barrage of lightning played out its drama in the large picture window, lighting up the living room's most impressive piece of furnishing, a massive floor-to-ceiling wall unit. A clutter of gadgets sat on the oak shelving, covered in dusty spider webs and insect carcasses. His father had always been the ultimate collector, never throwing anything away. Robots assembled from old artifacts sat with their mechanical arms dangling. Electronic eyes seemed to stare at Nick.

He turned around to see his father's blue eyes, the same color as his, all of a sudden light up.

"You're thinking why do I still have this stuff?"

"I remember when Mom joked about all your stuff being a Radio Shack on steroids. Back then, I didn't even know what she meant." Nick laughed at the memory.

"Yeah, Radio Shack. I used to shop there." Madison's voice was flat and humorless.

Nick pulled a chair next to his father's La-Z-Boy and sat down. His father tugged at a blanket, pulling it up over his knees, brushing away any attempts of assistance. Frost seemed to seep into the room and Nick shivered while his naturally curly hair frizzed in the humidity.

He listened to the rain bouncing off the window and remembered something his mother use to tell him when he was a child. He decided to break the silence and relieve the chill with the warmth of a favorite memory.

"I used to cry during storms because they frightened me. Tears and rain seemed to go together. Mom, always the optimist, had a spiritual way of looking at things. She would tell me 'rain was like Heaven's wet fingers' and I would remember her comforting, wet, soapy fingers dripping down on me when she bathed me as a child."

"You were such a momma's boy, so needy."

"Yeah, well, you weren't there when I needed you, Dad."

"When do you need to be at work?" Madison asked, looking at his watch.

"Always changing the subject when it gets too uncomfortable. I have a midnight shift. I have plenty of time... if you want me to stay?"

Nick looked at his father's drawn face and observed a sadness he never remembered seeing before.

"Are you alright, Dad?"

"Go on with your mother's story. I'm listening."

"Mom would say 'lightning was like Heaven's sparkling eyes.' She could look into your eyes and see into your soul."

"Your mother told me that my soul must have run off to join the circus, but since she liked going to the circus, she would bring it back to me. Sometimes your mother made no sense."

"Mom and I used to go to the circus. You had more important things to do. Laughter is good for your spirit, Dad, good for your soul." Nick gently laughed again. "So, did Mom ever bring it back?"

Sadly, Nick realized his mother's humor was lost on his father who took everything literally. His father could benefit from a little 'circus in his heart and in his soul.'

"Just continue with the story, already," Madison said while tapping his fingers along the chair's armrests.

"Whenever she heard thunder, she would call it 'Heaven's expressive voice' and she would laugh aloud, her voice full of life, an explosion of spontaneous excitement that was contagious. My laughter joined hers and I knew I had nothing to fear. She was a little bit of Heaven on Earth."

"Pretty story... but still think it's a bunch of nonsense... never could grasp Angie's beliefs. Science is all there is... you of all people should know that. There is nothing beyond that. Can't believe you held on to these tales all of these years."

All of a sudden, his father laughed, a strange guttural sound as if someone told a vulgar joke. Then he coughed and sputtered, pulled the blanket higher over his body, and closed his eyes. Soon all that could be heard was his snoring.

"I guess I'll be going," Nick said to his sleeping father.

He rushed out of the apartment and stepped out into the rain, the anger growing deep inside him, wanting to burst out.

"Why would you take her and leave him?" Nick screamed at the Heavens.

His tears became indistinguishable from the rain. He finally calmed down by the time he reached his car. Maybe it was easier to be like his father and not have emotions get in the way.

No. He was too much like his mother.

His upcoming midnight shift at the weather office reminded him of the connection he had with his father. They both had the same technical, mathematical, and scientific skills that were useful to an inventor and a meteorologist. There was no denying it; he was his father's son.

At midnight, a lightning bolt shaped like a hand with long, pointed fingers reached out from Heaven in search of its destination—the top of the roof over Madison's apartment building. It left a tiny smoldering hole, which the rain quickly extinguished. One lone bolt created an arc that struck a satellite dish in the same location directly over Madison's bedroom. The satellite dish glowed and sparked like a flying saucer, its outer rim charged with a bluish-white otherworldly neon ring of light.

Madison awoke to an explosion that shook his apartment. A few seconds later, the living room windows lit up with blinding white streaks of light.

A college memory filled his mind of taking lightning pictures from the top of the Old Observatory during the middle of a thunderstorm. Angie had stood next to him holding an umbrella over their heads. Static electricity would sing in the guy wires holding up a tall weather tower on the roof. He remembered his fearlessness, his obsession with weather.

Then another crash of thunder seemed to come from his deserted bedroom. He rose from his La-Z-Boy in a daze and nervously made his way there. He felt like he didn't belong or deserve to be going into this room, until the Door motioned him through with a "*hello, stranger,*" and he was on the other side. He rolled his walker over to an alcove where two winged chairs sat. Bluish misty light floated above the chairs and he looked up to see water filling the glass dome of a ceiling light fixture. Madison jumped with alarm as sparks flew out from the fixture. Water and electricity doesn't mix. What was going on here?

Then his cell phone vibrated in his pants pocket. Everything was coming alive at once.

Madison had never in his life, seen or felt anything like this.

It wasn't the phenomena called 'ball lightning' that he and Angie had once experienced in college. During that particular storm, they had watched through a window as sizzling whitish-blue electricity zigzagged along the top edge of a chain link fence. As it raced along, building up speed, it shot a rocket stream of intense blue light up toward the window. The light thickened into a grapefruit-sized orb. Madison and Angie sat mesmerized, as they watched this mystifying ball pass through the window with a popping sound. Amazingly, it did not break the glass. It hovered over them. Eventually, the ball lightning evaporated into the air, its whizzing sound fading away.

The sound of flowing water brought Madison's attention back to this new phenomenon. More sparks flew alongside a thin stream of water dripping onto the round glass table that sat between the chairs. He rushed to get a lavender vase to collect the water. When he placed it in the middle of the table, a voice rang out as a few sparks splashed into the vase.

"I have always loved that vase."

Madison shook his head trying to clear this new voice echoing through the room as he nervously paced.

"Madie, my love, you can't have doubts," Angie's ethereal voice broke through each spark.

"This is beyond my comprehension. Things do not work this way."

"It's just a step beyond math and science...everything is connected in the grand scheme of things."

Madison kept shaking his head and finally said, "It can't be true. First of all, this voice doesn't even sound like you... like my Angie ... the warmth is not there."

"Heaven and Earth's frequencies are not the same, you know."

"Like tuning in a radio signal?"

"It could be. I told them that a lightning storm could set everything in motion and grab your attention. I knew that you would need some proof. There had to be science behind it so I proposed using the satellite dish as a conduit for the ionization channels to project my voice through electrical sparks. Twa...laa—A conversation from Heaven."

"Angie, the science is not exactly perfect though I admit it has possibility, if I had a few more moments to analyze it, I would let you know if it has a scientifically sound premise. You keep mentioning 'them'? Who is helping you, and where are you? But most of all, I can't believe I am having this conversation. Angie, you died and left me, and now you're back trying to electrocute me."

"*Funny, Madie... The important thing is I've reached you. I know this whole thing is scaring you. Remember when Nickie was scared during a lightning storm? You both need to help each other now.*"

"I'm not scared. Do not compare me with Nick."

"*I miss you, but Heaven has surpassed my expectations because it reminds me of you ...a place filled with brilliance, a place that makes your heart sing with a selfish madness. I have been slightly cold lately, so looking for some Earthly warmth, to bring back the voice you remember. You're my little bit of Earth on Heaven and I will continue to watch you with great hope...I am counting on you, Madie.*"

Madison's voice grew tense, "What will I do, now?" He carefully moved closer to the dripping water, nervously sighed, and whispered, "All of these voices lately. It's just me and my madness."

The sparks stopped and there was silence.

"Angie, are you still here?"

A spark broke through the beads of water and he heard gentle laughter.

"*I'm always here. Heaven is closer than you think. You need to believe in yourself, Madie... take better care of yourself and reach out to our son. You both need each other, now more than ever. Remember when you see lightning, I'm not too far away. When you hear thunder, it's just me laughing.*"

Madison looked down at the water overflowing the lavender vase. The dripping from the ceiling fixture finally stopped. His cell phone was still vibrating. He pulled it out and it flashed 12:30. A mad thought went through his head. A thirty minute call from Heaven...what had just happened? Did he really talk with Angie? He could barely remember it. Now looking back at it, it seemed trivial, nonsensical, impossible, and unbelievable—he rattled off the list and looked at the cell phone that seemed to be agreeing with him.

"You need proof, Buddy. Without it, this new phenomenon is meaningless," it declared in a macho voice.

So many voices, but which ones to listen to, to believe in? The chatty radio, the bird on the windowsill, the macho cell phone, the welcoming door, and then his wife, Angie in Heaven. He was smart enough to understand that they all originated within him. Projecting his thoughts, his wishes, his beliefs into voices he heard.

"But what if..."Madison started to say with frustration to all of the voices that had been competing for his attention. "What if there is something out there, that is beyond math and science? Something I've been searching for throughout my whole life and never found."

For the first time since her death, he decided to sleep in their bed. A bolt of lightning streaked past the window, followed by thunder, and he instantly thought of Angie and warmth filled his soul. He gently laughed and felt more alive than he had for a long time. He remembered her cold voice in the sparkling water, so unlike her on Earth. Before falling asleep, he breathed into his cupped hands, whispered Angie's name, and hoped somewhere in Heaven that she was as warm as he was.

The rain gently fell throughout the night with an occasional lightning streak brightening the room. By 8:00 in the morning, another thunderstorm was moving into Miami Beach.

Madison picked up his cell and listened to the voice messages that his son had left throughout the night.

"Been worried about you, Dad. Shouldn't have left you alone...I knew you were not alright and then still left you. Why would I do that?"

Madison scrolled down the contact list, pressed his son's name, and waited.

"Hi, Nick, it's the end of your midnight shift. How about picking me up and we'll go out for breakfast?"

Over the airwaves, thunder boomed its agreement and both men laughed back.

The Lab Results are in

S. Ellen J.

Digitalization of Biopsies Returns Professional Diagnoses in Minutes

The lab's answer:
It's not cancer.

Everyone Gets a Puppy

Brian Cable

Pointy ears. Soft fur. Small mouth. Curious eyes.

Jeff wrote down "Ragmuffin" in the *Suggested Name* field. The puppy yawned, readjusted its position, and nestled its head down on top of its front paws.

A quiet noise came from the puppy's rear and he got a whiff of some foul chemical that the puppy's inner digestive system must have mixed up, like a chemist trying to find the right concoction to win in a battle against a skunk.

His nose scrunched up, and he wrote down "Ostentatious" in the *Desirable Family Demeanor* field. The conveyor belt started moving again, and the puppy was removed from Jeff's presence. Unfortunately, the conveyor belt was much less effective at removing its odor.

Even though his olfactory senses recoiled, the smell wasn't actually there with him. Nor was the conveyor belt. Or the puppy. They were all an Augmented Reality projection in Jeff's living room. He had *Ridin' on a Force Field* by *Anita Defenz* playing on his speakers, and a slice of bacon draped slightly over the edge of his plate that was perched on top of his coffee table.

To his surprise his own puppy, Lieutenant "Lute" Munchers, must not have noticed the bacon. If it had, it would have crawled across his lap in a

185

brave attempt to save Jeff from its greasy fats by snatching it and fleeing as fast as possible.

He was pretty sure puppies were still supposed to do that.

Another muffled noise came from down the hall, where his girlfriend, Mariah, was working. He could just make out the sound of an angry bark beyond her door. Lute perked up and looked down the hall.

Floppy ears. Cinnamon fur. Large canines. Three legged.

Jeff frowned. He didn't think they should have three legged animals, since they were so much harder to care for, but the higher-ups at Puppy Plant — the company he worked for — felt they were good for some families.

He hesitated for a moment, then marked down "Triceraflops" in the *Suggested Name* field.

The puppy looked intently at Jeff's hand. It seemed to be attracted to Jeff's pen. Just as the puppy was projected at him, so was his 3D image projected at the puppy's location.

Some would argue that the latter was totally unnecessary for the classification process, but Jeff disagreed. He felt that being able to see how the puppy reacted to him helped him make better recommendations.

He rubbed his chin for a moment, then wrote down "Charitable" in the *Desired Family Demeanor* field.

The conveyor belt started moving again. He glanced at his watch, and noticed Munchers was due for a walk. He reached out and grabbed the floating coffee icon and raised it up to signify his need to take a break. The conveyor belt image dispersed, and a bare wall greeted him.

"Oops." He didn't mean to dismiss it entirely. He grasped the floating paintbrush and said, "Home decor."

The bare wall was replaced with a scenic landscape, a river flowing out from under his sofa and turning into a waterfall two feet in front of him, and the walls of his apartment were replaced with a rock face, giving his living room the appearance of an elevated grotto.

Lute, lounging on the sofa and looking towards the virtual waterfall, squirmed a bit, then whimpered.

Jeff looked over at his pup, smiled, and patted it on its head. "Ready for a walk?" In response, Lute stretched its front paws, then leapt off the sofa into the rushing water — water that felt like carpet — and over to the door.

Or what would have been a door, if Jeff hadn't augmented such a boring slab of wood with a gnarly looking creature instead, his face with more creases than a hamper full of unwashed clothes. It stood as if guarding Jeff from the outside world.

The creature looked down at the puppy and its lips shifted into a smile, which looked as if an old fault line was grinding against itself and then finally broke free. "Forgetting something?" it said to Jeff.

Jeff raised his hand to show the leash that dangled from it. "I've been doing this a long time. You've got to do better than that." He took one end of the leash and tossed it towards Lute. It magnetically attached itself to Lute's collar. "Step aside, door troll."

"Couldn't you call me Rocky, just once?" asked the troll as it reluctantly shifted aside.

"You look more like a Jessica to me," said Jeff with a wink.

The door troll glared at him. "Let it be known you just winked at a door."

Jeff would have come up with some sort of witty reply if it weren't for Lute dashing out through the door and tugging at its leash.

"Hey buddy! Calm down." Jeff stumbled out the door behind Lute. Not good, he's supposed to represent his company and control his puppy better. He could ask them to give him a more well-behaved puppy, but he'd grown attached to the Lieutenant.

He quickly reached up and turned off the AR display. The waterfall and Rocky disappeared, along with the appearance that he was walking over nothingness, hundreds of feet above the ground below. A grassy front lawn, sidewalk, and street appeared in its stead.

He and Lute stopped just a few steps from the street. He glanced both directions and let out a sigh. That was close.

Lute found the sidewalk again and bounced from the grass on one side of the sidewalk to the other, poking its nose into the crevices and looking for tasty treats.

"Hey buddy, could you calm down so we can have a nice walk?"

Lute briefly stopped and looked up at him briefly, but then went back to sniffing the ground and tugging at its leash as it found a delicious looking piece of a discarded hamburger wrapper to investigate thoroughly with its nose. And tongue.

Jeff sighed. Lute shouldn't even go after trash. What was Mariah teaching these pups?

Lute suddenly stopped, and a light growl rose from within. Jeff saw his neighbor, Wallace, up ahead on the path. He wore the usual AR glasses everyone wore, a plain white tee-shirt, and a white pair of pants. Usually people wore all white when they liked to project some crazy outfit to other people's AR.

For a moment, Jeff wanted to turn around and lead Lute in the opposite direction, but he quieted that urge. He walked forward, giving Lute a light tug on the leash. Lute's growl increased, but it allowed Jeff to direct him towards the intruder.

Wallace had a small terrier puppy wandering around without a leash. Jeff had suggested he be named Scampalicious when the dog went through Classification, but Wallace had instead chosen T-Rex.

T-Rex investigated the yard, looking for a spot it hadn't adequately marked yet.

"You damn mutt, hurry up and go! I'm missing the game!" said Wallace. He kicked at the dog's nose, but T-Rex dodged out of the way and ran halfway down the block to put some space between it and Wallace.

Jeff tried to intervene. "You can't do that."

"The hell I can't!" said Wallace, turning his hateful eye to meet Jeff's. "It's mine, ain't it?"

"Yeah, but you're supposed to treat them well."

"I treat it fine." Two of Wallace's fingers pinched the air and moved towards his mouth. He inhaled sharply, held his breath for a moment, and then exhaled. "I'd treat it better if the Plant didn't make them so damn annoying."

"Puppies always take effort. Mine can be a handful too." As if on cue, he felt a tug from Lute as it strained its leash in an attempt to reach some berry it spotted on the ground. Or possibly rabbit poop. Hard to tell, as it went after both with equal fervor.

"I can say one thing about 'em, though. They're great for target practice." Wallace pointed his finger towards Lute. "Pow."

Jeff put himself between Wallace and his puppy. "Hey, cut it out!"

Wallace chuckled and shrugged. "Why? It didn't do nothing to him."

"But to you, you just shot him, didn't you? I bet there's blood spraying everywhere right now, from your perspective."

Another shrug. "I got all sorts of crazy crap going on here. They got this new app that makes people into zombies. It turns their skin white, their eyes yellow, puts blood all over their face. In fact," he leaned in closer, reached out, and made a brushing motion in front of Jeff's mouth, "I think you've got a little bit of brain sticking out of your mouth right now. Ever heard of a napkin?"

Jeff took a few steps back, and glared at Wallace. "Stop it. You're not supposed to aug when you're outside. You'll get yourself killed."

"I'm just outside for a moment, damn," said Wallace. "Why did I have to get the lame neighbor?" He looked behind him and said "T-Rex, come!"

From around the corner T-Rex came running towards its owner. He had no choice in the matter. It was compelled to do so. It saved the company money and was way too popular of a feature.

Wallace grabbed T-Rex by the scruff of its neck. The dog hung like a towel from a hook. A towel that wriggled. Wallace headed back inside his house. "Later."

The door slammed shut, and they were alone again. Jeff looked down at Lute. Lute looked at Jeff, then at the door, then back to Jeff again.

"I know, he's scary, isn't he?"

Lute growled quietly, then backed away.

Guess it's not going to go to the bathroom this time. Always happens when it gets scared. With a sigh, Jeff turned around and brought Lute back.

Once he reached his patio, he turned the AR glasses back on. The friendly face of the door troll reappeared to greet him.

"That was quick." Rocky stepped aside, his limbs making all sorts of cracking and creaking noises. "Forgot you had a delousing appointment? For you, I mean, not the little one."

As Jeff walked past he said, "Careful, or I'll make an appointment to delouse you."

"I think you got the words *delouse* and *delete* confused. Don't worry. It happens to everyone with a third grade vocabulary," said Rocky.

Jeff ignored the comment. "Shut the door."

"What, I don't get a wink this time? I was getting used to that." Rocky moved back into the doorframe.

The music was still playing, but had moved on to *Fresh off the Ship* by *Overshock*. *"We no longer fresh off the boat, we fresh off the space-ship. Whose ship? Our ship now, we jacked it! You backed it, they attacked it, up past the sky, we don't know why, let's all fly, before we all die! KA-BOOM! Son, I'm the only one, it's no fun when we run from the sun..."*

Jeff removed the leash from Lieutenant Munchers' collar, and the puppy promptly lived up to its name and ran to the kitchen to munch on some food from its bowl.

Pouring himself a glass of water, he returned back to the sofa, set the glass down, reached up for the coffee cup... and hesitated. He suddenly wasn't in the mood to get back to work.

Instead, he wandered down the hall. He knocked on his girlfriend's door, then heard Mariah say, "Come in. Just be careful."

He opened the door to her workspace. He shared a copy of Mariah's AR Vision for this room, so instead of a blank room, he saw a wide open space full of puppies, all Boxers, all sitting perfectly still, a few cocking their heads.

Well, except one, that was currently licking its private parts. That must be the actual one.

Mariah knelt next to it. She smiled back at Jeff, waved, then turned back to address her audience. "This will drive your future owners crazy. Lick here for about ten seconds, then leap up and smother them with kisses, then watch their bodies contort as they try to keep away from you. It's pretty funny, actually. Now you try."

The myriad of seated Boxers all suddenly started licking themselves. One licked itself in the armpit, another the end of its foot, another licked its chest, but most of the others were at least licking in the right general region.

"Good, good, keep it up." She got up on her feet and came up to embrace Jeff. "Hi, hun. What's up? Munchers acting up again?"

Jeff kissed her, then said, "Yes, but nothing I need you to fix. Can I pet the puppy?"

She loosened her grip on him and sighed, "Do you have to do this every time?"

Jeff nodded his head. "I mean, what's the point of dating a dog trainer otherwise, right?"

She rolled her eyes and fully separated from him. "His name is James."

"James? That's a boring name." Jeff knelt down before the puppy and ran his hands through his fur. James tried to lick him, and predictably, he backed away from the advances of James' tongue.

Coffee-colored. Strong shoulders. Thick jowls. Penetrating eyes.

Jeff stopped smothering James with petting and pretended to write something down. "Suggested name: Caramel Sanders."

Mariah knelt down next to them both, and said, "Well you are the resident expert. Caramel Sanders has been invaluable today. We've taught them how to stand on two legs to try to grab food off the table, how to step in poop immediately after going potty, and how to bark into people's ears. He's such a good teacher."

Jeff relinquished his hold on Caramel Sanders and leaned back on his hands. "Still don't quite get why teaching them bad behavior is supposed to make society better. They're robots, we could be making them behave for once."

The puppies in the background continued to lick themselves very inappropriately, not having been told any other commands by Mariah. They were currently in the obedience mode, where they followed every command as best as they could. It was a hidden feature that Puppy Plant disabled just before shipping them.

"Responsibility, humility, perspective. Doesn't sink in if they act like perfect angels."

"Wallace down the street has a brat of a puppy. I know because I classified it. But it doesn't make him any better. He just abuses it. Scampalicious is its name."

Mariah shrugged. "That's one reason why they don't get actual, living puppies. But overall, the mandate is working incredibly well. Less crime, less violence. And the more ornery we make them, the more useful they'll be."

Jeff placed a hand on her back and rubbed it gently. "I guess. It's just sometimes hard to remember when you've got proof it doesn't always work staring you down and scaring Lute every morning."

Mariah frowned. "There's something you should see." She reached up and grabbed a ball of yarn in front of her, and squeezed it lightly. It swiftly unraveled into a long strand, with small strands branching out and pictures with captions appearing at each, representing archives of video taken by the AR glasses. She touched the one that said 'Moving', and the ball quickly wound everything back up. A video appeared between him and herself. The screen showed a listing for their apartment, and then her saying "Hey babe! I found the perfect place for us!" from her point of view.

He remembered that text. Must have been a year ago, now.

She brushed her fingertips left to right across the video and it fast-forwarded. Lute appeared on the screen, and she stopped. "Lute's first walk when he got here."

Yeah, he remembered her excited messages about all the things he discovered on his walk. He had put off packing until the last minute, as usual, so he wasn't there to join them.

In the video, he could see Mariah look down at Lute, and say, "Isn't this exciting! A whole new area for you to explore! Lots of trees, grass fresh air, ... yes and new poop to smell, good boy!"

On screen, Lute sniffed absolutely everything in his path, and strained to reach places far off the sidewalk.

As they rounded the corner, Lute stiffened up, stopped moving, and whined. Mariah looked up and saw a puppy lying on its side in the front yard. Except it wasn't relaxing. The fur on its head had a hole where its fur split was open, and the electronics underneath were exposed.

Jeff gasped. The puppy was Scampalicious.

Mariah wore a grim look like a shroud across her face. "It gets worse."

On the screen, Mariah had rushed towards the dog and pulled out an AR enhancer, a transparent screen that magnified the image and analyzed what it saw, and started checking its head.

Until she heard a, "Hey! What do you think you're doing?" She looked up to see Wallace, lounging in a chair on his patio, holding a pistol and gesturing to her with it.

She stood up. "Sir, is this your puppy? You realize you just committed a crime, right?"

Wallace growled, "It's just a fine. No big deal. Snatched a slice of pizza off my plate. Damn thing can't eat, but steals food anyway. Good pizza too. Sausage to die for."

"How dare you! Killing something over pizza!"

He stopped using the pistol as a gesture and instead pointed it towards Lute. "You're right. Much better I kill for something I can't get fined for. Like being on my property."

Lute's deep growl morphed into a sharp, loud, incessant bark at Wallace. He strained in his leash to go towards him. Mariah forcibly pulled him away.

Wallace fired.

The bullet embedded itself in the ground next to Lute. Lute jumped back, while Mariah stiffened.

Wallace smirked and said. "I don't miss. My next shot won't either."

She ran back towards the house, and brought Lute inside. She locked everything up, sat down for a moment, and then called Puppy Plant. "'Hello, I'd like to report a Mistreatment—

Mariah made a crumpling gesture and the video folded into itself and disappeared. "Now you know why I insisted we walk all the dogs in the other direction for the first few months."

"That's insane," said Jeff. "Why wasn't he arrested? And why are we still living in the same city as that monster?"

Mariah shrugged. "The company knows these kinds of things will happen, and just sends some maintenance guys to fix or replace the puppy, then charge the owners for doing so. They still can't escape the mandate, at least not without paying out the nose for it."

"I— how come you never mentioned this?"

"I didn't want to worry you. Besides, you found out for yourself just how bad he was soon enough. My point is, he's gotten better, it's just been gradual over time."

Jeff sighed. "I guess. Instead of actual guns he just uses virtual ones now. Doesn't seem like a big improvement to me."

"It doesn't have to work miracles for absolutely everyone. But it is working overall. There's plenty of other people out there where the results are even more dramatic."

"I guess."

A loud bark came from the living room. Jeff gave Mariah a quick peck and said, "Lute probably needs some food. I should feed him, then — I guess I'll get back to work."

"Okay, hun. I'll take a break in a bit and we can make lunch."

"Sounds good." He kissed her again, and went back to the living room, to discover Lieutenant Munchers perched on an arm of the couch with a ball in its mouth. It wagged his tail while shifting its feet to keep its balance. Jeff smiled, and said, "Alright, we'll play fetch, but just a briefly. Then I have to get back to work."

As he walked in and reached to grab the ball, Lute spun around and farted right into his outstretched hand.

Jeff laughed. When had Mariah taught him to do this? Maybe it encouraged greater responsibility, by forcing him to be careful where he reaches? Seemed like a stretch, though. He wrestled with Lute for the ball, then tossed it across the room.

Love Letters From Space

Diana Jean

I used to think that zero gravity would be
like water but water is weight
and currents, pulling and pushing.
Today, I blinked a tear from my eye,
saw it travel into the halo of your hair,
you turned and rubbed your sleeve
on my eyes, scattering my tears like space dust.
Zero gravity has no current,
but it managed to pull me to you

A hundred years ago Earth
saw The Pillars of Creation
destroyed by a supernova
arriving six thousands years
late on the speed of light. Now we travel
to the star SM123-43
watch it supernova in fast forward.
You waited in the airlock with me,
your visor shield reflecting the dying
star's white, blue, and stunning
hydrogen explode into the nebula.

You said that if we traveled back,
the star would turn back too,
the Pillars of Creation would reform
and we could be inspired
by the beauty again.
I touched your visor,
my gloved fingers bulky and stiff. I traced
the outline of a star dying,
a star giving birth
over your lips and told you I needed
no other beauty to inspire me.

I felt the gravity with you
on a planet twice the density of Earth.
We slogged along the dusty ground,
gasping and laughing. I collected
a sample of pure silicon,
shining in the blue starlight
and watched it float in our ship's cabin,
reflecting the lights in your smile and laugh.
I felt the gravity with you
on a moon where we could jump
over the landing pod without effort.
You jumped before me,
your outline only visible
in the landing lights.
The nearest star too far
to be more than another speck
in the void. I followed you,
feeling my stomach rise
as I sailed over. You were there,
on the surface of frozen methane

shimmering in our lights
reaching for me as I fell.

There is so much emptiness
in space. Places where
it is dark, places where
stars' lights travel millions
of years through places where
there has never been sound
or warmth or even a molecule
of carbon, hydrogen, helium.
There is nothing there to see us,
in those places.
Nothing but the humming
of our engines, the ambient lights.
Your hands were warm in those cold pockets
of space, your breath,
your whisper was loud
in that emptiness
you pulled me close and kissed me
in that silence
I told you that if my body were to
supernova and everything were to spill out
I would fill a nebula with stars bright
enough to shine in every
corner of this universe
and I would expand every
light-second with my love for you.

How the First Chickens Got to Mars

Yolanda Huslig

The ships from Earth arrived on our Martian plain yesterday. We wait, Dad and I, in the big conference room with its bare block walls, empty except for ninety people, half the population of Plymouth. A low hum pervades the room. Marika, my friend in Maquon, the other village on Mars, texts me they are waiting too. Getting something physical from Earth is special.

We watch the double doors leading to the garage where packages are unloaded from the rover that meets the ships. Kuval, short, dark, and skinny, bangs his way through the double doors using a cart loaded with boxes, shipping envelopes and bags. He parks it in the middle of the room. Kuval is old. He tells stories of those first sols on Mars, 27 Earth years ago. It took awhile for the colonists to adjust. Sols are longer than Earth days by 39 minutes. Kuval reads names and hands out packages.

One of the double doors opens. The mayor, my Mom, and two strangers walk in. Mom, tall and fair skinned, grew up in Canada. Everyone calls her "Ruth" even though she's the mayor. She keeps the Intranet running and connected to Earth's Internet. The door flaps shut after them.

Samir, my Dad, is shorter and darker than Mom. Born in Iraq, he has a PhD in exo-biology and came to Mars to look for indigenous life. He's a farmer now. I'm tall, like Mom, and dark, like Dad.

I lean toward Dad. "Those people look strange, pudgy like pillows."

Dad nods, his face grave. "Well fed."

Mom looks gaunt next to them.

The mayor says, "I'd like to introduce two new colonists, Asher and Megan. Asher is an energy expert. Megan is a hairdresser. Please welcome them."

Several people push forward, others follow, some with outstretched hands, and mill around the strangers.

Kuval empties the first cart and brings in the second before he calls my name. "Elise."

I move forward. Seven Earth months ago when the supply ships left Earth, Granddad sent a video telling me to expect a package.

Kuval drops a large, square-ish box into my hands.

It's heavy. It's big. Even with outstretched arms, my chin rests on top. I move back by Dad, set it on the floor, and look at the tag. It says "Happy 14th and 15th Birthdays." I giggle. On Earth I would be 15. Here on Mars I'm 8. Dad piles the other packages and letters we receive on top.

We have to wait for a cart. There are only five. When we finally have one and have it loaded, Mom is gone and so are Asher and Megan.

We wheel the cart out the main door, up the ramps two levels, and down the door-lined corridor to our quarters. After we unload, he returns the cart.

While he's gone, I take the box into my room and open it, just to peek. The parts don't make sense to me. I take out the bill of lading, put it in my pocket, and head for the kitchen area without reading it. I have to get dinner started.

––––––––––––––––

Dinner is ready and the table set but Mom isn't home yet. I hold the potatoes in the oven and watch the beans simmer on the stove, grinding my teeth. "Mom's never late for dinner."

"She's mayor now. She has responsibilities." Dad sits at the dinner table, fidgeting with a long, thin, green leaf.

Mom walks in, thirty minutes late. "I told them no more settlers this year."

We'd heard it before. Potatoes and beans go to the table.

"I asked for solar cells, maybe a small nuclear reactor or two, and extra food. They sent people instead." Mom paces. She turns to Dad. "How are the crops?"

"Most, like the potatoes and rutabagas, are fine."

"Beans?"

"We should have a good harvest."

"That new crop, it's a grain crop, isn't it?"

Dad nods. "Wheat."

"How's it doing?"

Dad shakes his head. "Not good. The leaves are pale. Something's been eating it."

Mom's eyebrow rises. "On Mars?"

"That's what I thought. But..." Dad taps the leaf. The edges are jagged and misshapen, the tip chewed off.

Mom runs a finger along the leaf's edge. She sighs and slides into a chair. "What did my father send you, Elise?"

I take the bill of lading out and spread it on the table. "Twelve fertile chicken eggs, an incubator with backup battery, chicken feed, a waterer and directions for the incubator." My heart starts to race. Real birds! Like the birds he's been telling me about forever.

Mom blinks. The only eggs in the colony are the powdered kind.

"Eggs would spoil during the seven month trip," Dad says.

"They're frozen."

"What are you going to do with them?" Mom asks.

"Um." My hands turn clammy. What if they wouldn't let me? "Try to hatch them. That's what Granddad sent them for."

—

Marika walks over the hill from Maquon to help me put the incubator together and install the eggs. The incubator produces a warm glow that lights my room and warms my heart. I turn off the regular light to conserve energy.

"Twenty-three days until we have chickens," I say.

"What are chickens good for?" Marika asks.

"Laying real eggs."

"What else?"

"Eating."

"And?"

Marika has a point. The more benefits they provide the more likely I can keep them.

"Maybe there's something on the Intranet." I poke around on my tablet. "Nope. Nothing."

"On Earth's Internet?" Marika asks.

"Probably." I frown at my tablet. You can find anything on the Internet. It's so convenient, for Earth people connected by fiber optic cable. Relying on electromagnetic waves when you're millions of miles away makes it take forever.

"What's wrong?"

"I don't have time for this. I'll ask Granddad to send me information on chickens."

The next day my computer chimes during English class alerting me I'd received a message from Granddad. The class could wait. I pause it and open the email.

"Sorry I didn't send an instruction manual. I found an e-book that covers the care and feeding of chickens. It should download to your tablet within the next day or two. Chickens are good eating. So are their eggs."

On sol fourteen, I'm home alone turning the eggs when someone knocks on the front door. The directions say to turn them three times a day. Three times a sol better be enough. I answer the door. Asher, the new guy, stands outside. A little shorter than I am, he has a beak of a nose that makes him look predatory.

"I'm with the Energy Division. I've come to inspect your energy systems," Asher says.

"My parents aren't home. Can you come back later?"

Asher sticks his foot inside the door. "It'll only take a minute."

"You don't have the right to come into my house without my permission." I put my hand on his chest and shove. He doesn't move.

"I work for the Company. That's permission enough." Asher shoves me back into the room and steps inside. Starting at the kitchen, he checks every outlet and appliance we have, opening cabinets and looking behind furniture. He pulls out his phone and makes notes. I follow, protesting. He ignores me. I pick up my tablet to text Mom and Dad. He grabs it out of my hands. Finished with the front room he moves on to Mom and Dad's room, the bathroom, then my room.

"What's this?" Asher points at the incubator.

I tell him.

"It isn't an accepted use of power." Asher pulls the plug. The backup battery takes over.

I reach over to plug the incubator back in.

Asher grabs my wrist and pulls me around. "Don't, or we'll turn all the power off to this unit."

"Ow." My wrist smarts where he grabbed it. "The eggs won't stay at the right temperature. They won't hatch." I jerk my wrist out of his hand and blink back tears.

"No wonder the mayor keeps asking for more energy systems. You waste it." Asher hands me my tablet and walks out the front door, saying over his shoulder. "We'll be monitoring this unit for extra power use."

I glare at the closed door. The skunk.

Back in my room, I finish turning the eggs and then pull out the directions for the incubator. It has a four hour battery life. I check amperage requirements for the incubator and all our appliances and add them up.

We aren't using more than our allotment, even with the incubator.

Shaking with rage, I grab my tablet, pull up the village website, and fill out the request for variance asking for a higher energy allotment for ten days, mark it urgent, and send it in. I also file a complaint against Asher for trespassing.

I receive the approved variance the next day. At the next village meeting, where the citizens meet to decide on important issues, I stand up and describe how Asher trespassed. The villagers are lenient with Asher, since he is new here and it is a first offense, explaining that the Company does not have the right to enter our private quarters without a warrant.

On sol twenty-two I hear cheeps coming from one of the eggs. The directions say to cheep back. So I do. When the first chick pecks the first hole in its egg, I text Marika. We round up all the school aged children in both Plymouth and Maquon and bring them over to watch the birds hatch. Mom arranges to work from home that day.

We move the incubator to the front room. Sixteen children running in circles and laughing fill our quarters to overflowing. Marika sits in front of the incubator. When she calls out that a chick has pecked its first hole in its shell the children stand around it, mesmerized until they get bored. When one chick finally opens the shell all the way, the children stop to watch the chick pull itself out of the shell and lay there, tired, its feathers drying.

Two days later, I have seven light reddish brown puffs running around inside the incubator, cheeping. The unhatched eggs go into the community compost bin.

I send Granddad pictures of the new chicks.

Granddad responds.

"Seven of them hatched. That's great! The new freezing procedure sometimes kills the little embryos inside the egg. But this was the best way I could find to send you fertile eggs."

When the chickens outgrow the incubator I move them to a pen in the front room. It works better, especially when a friend or neighbor stops by to check on them.

At eight weeks, the chickens have feathers. I pick up the last bag of feed from under the pen and frown. Lifting it is way too easy. I can't put off addressing the feed issue any longer. Opening the pen, I lean in and feed and water the chickens. Finished, I close and latch the lid and put the feed bag away. Dad said the feed might grow if planted, depending on what's in it, but not fast enough to feed the chickens.

Watching the chickens run around and peck and try to fly makes me laugh. I've grown fond of them.

I pick up my tablet to login to math class. Instead, I open the e-book Granddad sent me. It says chickens are omnivores. They can eat grain but their best treats are insects. Not many of those here. Our largest crop is potatoes. There are barely enough of those for the humans. Food scraps? We compost those. How big a dent would feeding my seven chickens food scraps make in the compost piles? Not much, I would imagine. Besides, they're contributing their poop to the piles.

I talk with the kids in Plymouth. They are eager to help with the chickens. Soon, I have a thriving food scrap collection ring going. When I tell Marika, she organizes the kids in Maquon to join the ring.

At twenty weeks, Dad comes home from the fields holding a mesh bag he tosses on the counter. "I found out what's been eating the wheat plants."

Mom picks up the bag and holds it flat in her hand. Visible through the mesh is an inch long brownish bug with large hind legs.

"It's dead. I didn't use a pressure box to bring it in," Dad used pressure boxes to bring produce in from the field when he didn't want it to freeze or desiccate in Mars's thin atmosphere.

"Grasshoppers." Mom puts the bag down. "They can't have come from Mars."

"No, but the only new non-Mars thing in that field is the seed."

"Could it be the seed?"

"Seems odd."

"I'll ask where the Company got the seed they sent us," Mom says.

"What do they do on Earth about pests?" I ask.

"Use pesticides," Dad says.

"That's out. We can't afford to poison our soil," Mom says.

"I could deflate the dome."

"We'd lose the wheat, too."

At twenty-one weeks I return from a day in Maquon to find the chickens roaming around loose in our quarters. I put the bag of food scraps in the refrigerator, my tablet on the computer table and turn to the chickens.

"How did you guys get out?" The lid on their pen leans up against the wall. I'd closed and latched it this morning. They'd been out for a while, too. Chicken poop peppers the floor, with some on the dining table.

I start chasing chickens. Soon, six chickens are in the pen. The seventh is nowhere to be seen. Did it get out the front door somehow? No one locks their doors in Plymouth. There doesn't seem to be a need. Anyone could walk in to check on the chickens. But why let them out? Did the seventh chicken sneak out when they left?

I wander up and down the corridor knocking on neighbor's doors asking if they'd seen my chicken. When I get to Asher and Megan's door, Megan answers.

"Come on in, child," Megan ushers me into her quarters. She seems unusually happy. "Look what my wonderful Asher found." She points to the stove.

Megan doesn't give me a chance to speak. She calls me 'child' even though I'm as tall as she is and she isn't that much older than me.

"We've been starving since we've been here. Tonight we're going to eat chicken." Megan opens the oven door. Inside is a chicken bereft of its feathers, head and feet, belly up, the naked skin turning a golden brown.

I gasp and cover my mouth. "That's my chicken."

"Your chicken, child? Why Asher bought it at the store," Megan chuckles.

"You stole my chicken!"

The smile vanishes from Megan's face. "This chicken is from the store. Your chickens are a nuisance. They stink."

"They don't stink." I blink back tears. I don't want Megan to see me cry. I swing my fist at her face as hard as I can.

She grabs my wrist before it lands. "Get out of my house!" She throws me out onto the floor of the corridor, and slams her door.

Dazed, I stare at her door. No one stole anything on Mars. There was nothing to steal. Presently, I drag myself up and go home. The place is a mess. I sit down at the computer table. Taking a deep breath, I pick up my tablet and file a complaint at the village website.

I clean the chicken poop off the table, sweep and wash the floor while tears stream down my face. I never felt so violated in my life.

Mom gets home while I'm washing the floor. She takes one look at my face. "What's wrong?"

"They're eating my chicken," I sniffle.

"What? Who?" Mom looks confused.

Dad walks in. I tell them both what happened.

Mom's jaw sets and her eyes sparkle with anger. She sits down at the family computer and pounds away. Finished, she turns to me. "The next village meeting is now scheduled for sol after tomorrow. Be ready to explain your complaints. Your chickens will also be on the agenda. Megan is right. Your chickens do stink. We're starting to get complaints."

———————————

At the village meeting I stand up front and explain how Asher unplugged the incubator and Asher and Megan stole my chicken. I tell them chickens could provide fresh eggs and meat. Mars citizens don't take stealing lightly. They decide on community service hours, 100 for Megan and 200 for Asher. They give me a week to find a better place for the chickens.

I mull over what to do with the chickens for a couple of sols. Finally, I ask Dad if I can put them in the wheat field. He says yes, the grasshoppers have doomed it anyway. Mom and Dad help me get them there.

The next time Marika visits I take her to the wheat field. I wave at Kuval, on top of the dome, sweeping dust off. The pressure suits of the two people helping him are unmarked. Six chickens wander among the rows of calf-high wheat inside the dome. Outside, on one side, are dirt and rocks and dunes. On the other another dome filled with green leaved plants. Marika stands in the field and turns around. "Neat," is all she says.

Two people in unmarked pressure suits barge through the airlock. Neither takes the time to blow the dust off before coming inside. Both whip off their helmets. Megan rushes at me. Asher tries to stop her.

"This is the girl who lodged that ridiculous complaint against us." Megan points at me. "That's why we're out here sweeping dust off the domes."

"Now, Megan," Asher says.

"You can't prove that chicken was yours," Megan says.

"Megan, calm down." Asher tries to grab her arm but she fights him off.

"It could be from anywhere. I'm sure with the village's lax rules against livestock there are chickens all over."

"There aren't any others," I say.

"Maybe it's from Maquon," Megan says.

"No one in Maquon has live chickens," Marika says. "I know. I live there."

"There has to be a poultry farm somewhere on Mars," Megan says.

"No, there isn't," I say.

"Then where did you get yours?" Megan asks.

"My Granddad sent them to me," I say. "Why did you take one?"

Mom and Dad slip through the airlock. Mom waves to Kuval perched on top of the dome.

Megan sighs. "No meat. No fresh fruit. I can't wait to go back to Earth."

"Earth?" My eyes bug out. I can't help it.

Megan nods. "I don't want to live in such a backward place. Asher, we're going back on the next available space ship."

"I'll see to it." Asher whips out his phone and swipes it. He taps in a number and wanders off mumbling.

Dad and Mom sidle toward us, listening.

Marika's jaw hangs open. I shake my head. "Don't you know?"

"Know what?" Megan asks.

"There are no spaceships going from here to Earth," I say.

Asher returns yelling into the phone. "You gotta be kidding me."

I shake my head. Didn't they know before they came?

"Why those double-crossing swine." Asher walks in circles looking upward at the dome, clutching his phone. "They tricked me."

Megan stares at him wide-eyed.

"They promised me a big promotion and large raise if I would come and help the colonists with their energy problems. No one said anything about a one-way trip."

"They never mentioned it on the videos about us?" I ask.

"The videos about the Mars colonists? That's so passe," Megan says. "Nobody watches those anymore."

Mom reaches my side. She confronts Megan and Asher. "You two have community service hours. Get your helmets on and go."

Asher eyes Mom. When she reaches for her phone he picks up his helmet. "Come on, Megan. We're almost done for today."

They put their helmets on and leave.

Dad runs a finger under a leaf.

A chicken snags a grasshopper out of the air and swallows it.

"Did you see that?" I ask. "I didn't know chickens liked grasshoppers."

Another chicken catches another grasshopper.

"If chickens eat grasshoppers, can humans eat them, too?" Marika asks.

Mom says. "Some people eat them fried."

Looking down the rows of wheat, I spot a place where the leaves are matted down. "What did my chickens do?"

I run down the row to see. On top is a brown egg, just like the eggs I'd gotten in the mail.

"Marika! Dad! Mom! Over here!" I wave.

"What?" Marika asks.

I hold the egg up. "Look."

Dad laughs. "One of your hens laid an egg."

"Will it hatch if I put it in the incubator?"

"Only if a rooster was there to fertilize it. Either way they could be gold here on Mars," Dad says.

"If I have a rooster?"

"You could grow more chickens," Mom says.

"These chickens are eating the grasshoppers that are eating the wheat in this field. They're useful for that alone," Dad says.

A chicken crows.

Mom looks up. "Maybe you have a rooster."

I smile.

Afterword

Author Bios and Inspiration

The Writing Journey

Barbara Bartilson

Barbara is a new author to the Journey anthology writers and invites you to enjoy her short story. "Remember the Ladies" is speculative fiction with a foundation in American history, the values we hold, and Akashic Records from a rarely-referenced storehouse of knowledge.

Her other writing experience has been in business where she consults and leads large-scale strategic corporate change. She uses creative writing skills to construct business cases, organizational change recommendations, and other position papers to plan and build desirable future-states. She can be reached at *https://www.linkedin.com/in/barbara-bartilson-2924234*

She thanks the Naperville Writing Group and others for their perspectives and critiques and especially Mary O'Brien Glatz for editorial encouragement and extraordinary ability to help see a way forward!

Inspiration: Abigail Adams

Abigail Adams was strong-willed, intelligent, and a true partner to the founding fathers of the United States of America. What would she say about the current state of the union? What would she say about women's roles? She ran her own business and investments in Massachusetts while her husband lived out-of-town and overseas for much of their marriage.

How would she interpret the presidential election in 2016? What would be her strategy going forward?

Bonnie B. Bradlee

Emerging from a life deep in the depths of drug and alcohol abuse in 2005, Bonnie began pursuing her dream of writing. A lifetime of journaling and short story writing finally comes to fruition in this anthology, her first ever published stories. As a credentialed pastor within the Assemblies of God, a majority of her writing revolves around redemption and stories of hope. She is also pursuing completion of a novel consisting of a modern version of an Old Testament Biblical story.

Inspiration: Talitha and Paulie

Both of these stories involve the Great Perhaps. Several years ago, Bonnie's grand niece posted a photo on Instagram with the caption "I go to seek a Great Perhaps." Being intrigued by the statement, Bonnie investigated and learned that these were the last words of the 16th century philosopher, François Rabelais. Look for future stories from Bonnie, based on the same theme.

Elaine Fisher

Since 2013, Elaine Fisher has been a member of the Writing Journey and has two published short stories, "Corpse Du Jour" and "Metamorphosis" in the 2015 Journey anthology, *Voices from the Dark*. She also has a flash fiction piece and a poem in the 2016 Journey online anthology, *Human*. Her most recent work, the short story "Stepmothers" and poem "The Key Maker," is in the 2017 Journey Anthology, *Near Myths*.

Each November, for the past five years, Elaine has completed a first draft novel during National Novel Writing Month. Her favorite Nano novel has turned into a YA historical fantasy series called *The Dream Travelers* about two teenage girls, one from the present time and one from the Old West, who exchange places.

Inspiration: Playback

Magical realism seemed to be a good genre for this flash fiction piece especially given the speculative aspect behind this anthology. I asked myself -"what if ...we could live our lives going backwards instead of forward?' For the elderly, the chance to 'relive' their past might be a happier, more hopeful direction for some of them to go.

My main character is an elderly photographer who orders a magical memory card hoping it can 'play back' lost, forgotten memories. I used photography terms throughout the story. I liked the symbolism equating the human eye to the camera lens. The word, "light" can be interpreted in both technical and spiritual ways such as letting the "light" into the lens of the camera or "seeing the light."

Inspiration: The Lightning Chamber

This short story's genre has supernatural and sci-fi elements to it. I wondered -'what if...there was a connection between the scientific world and the spiritual world we live in?' These two worlds and the people who are part of them seem to be as opposite as they could possibly be. What does it take to be a believer? Is there a Heaven? Do we need physical proof, or is faith enough? Maybe it is as simple as first having faith in ourselves by discovering our inner feelings and beliefs and then hopefully being able to share these ideas with others. But can people be open to new ways of looking at things, understanding things? I hope so.

All of the stories I tend to write are character-driven, in this case, a story of a father and son, told through both of their POVs. The father is an eccentric old inventor and his adult son is a meteorologist. Other characters are the 'voices' that the inventor hears including his dead wife who helps to mend the estranged relationship between her husband and their angry son. The 'weather' plays an important character in this story as well.

Mary O'Brien Glatz

Mary O'Brien Glatz has been writing forever, but only since she retired from a career as an Educational Psychologist has she given herself time to write fiction. She is grateful to The Lighthouse in Denver, Colorado, where she took writing courses with well known authors and great teachers. Most of her fiction springs from her real life experiences. She has published a memoir in the Creative Nonfiction genre, *Anywhere But Here: A First Generation Immigrant Life*, and has published short stories through The Writing Journey in Anthology 12 *On Being Human* and in Anthology 13, *Near Myths*. She is currently working on producing and editing her own collection, *Dreaming You Alive - Women in Love, Loss, Life*.

Inspiration: The Clearing

Magical realism is a natural response to disaster. When it appears that all hope is lost; when the future indeed looks dark; and when we feel as if we have no control over reality; a turn to the mystical, magical, spiritual, and to internal contemplation and reflection, can be a healing balm. Sometimes redefining, expanding, and reimagining reality is the most we can do. Real people and real events inspired the characters in this story. The story depicts an actual personal experience of a shamanic clearing and, yes, the results of the 2016 election. The political is the personal and the personal is political. What impacts one of us impacts all of us. We are awake and out of our trance now.

Todd Hogan

Todd Hogan is a Chicago writer whose work has been published in the anthologies Stories from Other Worlds, Voices from the Dark, Human: An

Exploration of What It Means, and Near Myths, and will appear in the new anthology from Write-On Joliet.

Yolanda Huslig

Yolanda Huslig escaped the corporate world by retiring after thirty years as an engineer. To pursue a lifelong dream, one that had been put on hold in the hustle and bustle of life, she enrolled in a creative writing course. Eight semesters later, she'd learned how to write a story. She continues to hone her craft, writing, reading and attending workshops. She writes mainly science fiction, the kind that could actually happen.

Inspiration: How the First Chickens Got to Mars

The idea of living and working in space has always intrigued me. I wonder what living on Mars would be like at the time of the first colonists, before they start terraforming the planet. What would it be like for their children? What would they eat? Where would it come from? For example, would they have chickens? If they did, how would the chickens get to Mars? In this story, Elise's grandfather sends her frozen chicken eggs. They hatch into cute little brown puffs. But they grow up into noisy, smelly birds.

Diana Jean

Diana is a twenty-something-something who spends most of her day writing or making excessively frilly dresses. She also enjoys Disney, bubble baths, espresso, Star Trek, Harry Potter, fried chicken, pink, lavender, cabernet sauvignon, and watching the mess in her space grow to hoarding levels.

You can reach Diana Jean at
DianaJean0416@gmail.com (DianaJean0416 at gmail dot com)
, find more of her novels and short stories at her *Goodreads*, or follow her *blog*.

Inspiration: Shotai's Song

Much fiction about space travel revolves around danger or climatic moments. I decided to write something more 'domestic'; a cleaning robot's daily life of programmed tasks, making friends, and discovering new things. I also wanted to explore the concept of a main character, unable to make make many sounds, learning how to 'sing'.

Inspiration: Love Letters From Space

There is a certain infinite loneliness in space; a vast emptiness that is almost inconceivable. Yet, I think we have always managed to find love and beauty in places that seem so completely inhospitable. These are not only love letters to another human exploring the great unknown, they are also love letters to the universe itself.

Debra Kollar

Debra Kollar is a writer of several different genres. Whether she is writing a humorous fiction piece or an interview for the newspaper she tries to keep one thing consistent, her voice. She believes everyone in her writings—real or imaginary—has their own truth to tell. Debra is a graduate of Purdue University. Her work has appeared in several newspapers, an art exhibit on diversity and in six anthologies.

Inspiration for Step Right In

We live in a world where mental issues and emotional pain are overlooked and dismissed. The idea for this story came from watching a friend's bravery in trying every imaginable cure to help her depression. In fact, there are many people in this world trying to get close to that sunlight mentioned in the story. People trying to feel like a part of this world when on the inside they most definitely don't. How great would it be, how absolutely wonderful, if we could cure depression, PTSD, anxiety, trauma, OCD, bipolar, schizophrenia, acceptance of self, grief or guilt from a loved one's death—all in one night. Everyone deserves their place in the sunlight.

Tanasha L. Martin

Tanasha Martin has written poetry from a very young age and wrote her first short story, "top pick" for a creative writing competition in 1990. She first participated in NanoWriMo in November 2015, drafting her first Young Adult Science Fiction novel. Since then, she has been writing full-time and in 2016, completed the first draft of a Young Adult Fantasy Series. Poetry, flash fiction, short stories, children's books and Sci-Fi and Fantasy novels are among her works in progress. The region features a writing community called the *Writing Journey*; Tanasha is the author of several works in the 2016*Anthology 12 and Anthology 13 of the Writing Journey*: *Near Myths (A Tale with No Fairies, Everglow, and The Scant Structure Slayers)* and *Human: An Exploration of What It Means (Touched, Personal Bubble, and All Smiles)*.

Tanasha is a Member of Society of Children's Book Writers and Illustrators.

Inspiration: Peer

The rationale, processes, and arguments behind cloning has always been of interest to me. The idea of someone in the world, a carbon copy of you, a true "peer" is a fascinating idea. How alike or different would we truly be? Would we be considered family? What if I had a disability and it was corrected in making my clone? Would we still be viewed by ourselves or others as "peers"? I was curious what it would be like to "peer" into the lives of both the clone and the "original" in that situation. How would they view one another? Would they see who they could become? Would they see the potential in what they could become to one another?

Inspiration: Once More, With Feeling

Recently there has been talk in the scientific community about computers creating poetry, stories, music, paintings, etc., that is "just as good" as those that are a product of human creativity. This story is an exploration into why that idea and experimentation bothers me. I believe that the fine arts reflect a conversation between people - a sharing of feeling, ideas, and experiences. It is a conversation that lifts and inspires us within the human condition. If our lives are devoid of these conversations, will our individual and/or collective creativity be affected? Will we lose our ability to speak to others in our own unique ways? Will it stifle us in our progress as a human race?

Inspiration: Digital Footprint

Social media is a large part of our lives today. It is where we spend a good deal of our down time, our work life, and it displays to the world who we are or who we would want the world to think we are. But does it really? Social media can sometimes be a place of insecurity, frustration, bitterness, and hatred. If you were given the opportunity to view yourself - your profile on social media - would you be proud of the person displayed there? What if it were the *only* information you or anyone had about you? Is that persona the impression about yourself that you would want a new world to know? Would you want to return to life as that person?

Annerose Walz

Annerose Walz is a writer and photographer, and a lot more in between. She writes mostly young adult fiction and short stories.
Six years ago Annerose moved with her family to the United States of America. Taking some time off to help her family adjust to the changes, she also refocused on her true love - creativity. Annerose bought a camera and started to pursue photography, design, and writing. Beside capturing the outside world with her camera she cannot help but to write about

the various creatures who exist in her inner world demanding to be freed from the depth of her brain.

Annerose Walz wrote for numerous newsletters and non-fiction articles for non-profit organizations, but her real love is fiction writing. Presently, she is writing her first YA series and short stories.
Her short story, *Wolf's Legacy* appears in the Writing Journey Anthology 12, *Near Myth*.
You can find more information at *www.AnneroseWalz.com*

Inspiration: Lost on the South Lawn

An asteroid called 2004 MN4 will pass the Earth in April 2029. NASA keeps a close eye on its trajectory. The Arecibo Observatory in Puerto Rico predicted in 2005 that this asteroid will pass the Earth within about 30,000 miles of the Earth's center. A collision in 2029 is still ruled out.

I wondered what would happen if this trajectory would change and the calculation would show that the asteroid would hit the Earth or our moon.

How would the States of this Earth handle this situation? Would they be able to work together and prevent doom's day? Would they be able to set aside all the differences in culture, race and religion and work together for the greater good?

Greg Wright

Greg is an author of short stories and adult fiction. With degrees in Horticulture and Soils, and an MBA, he now writes in his free time. His short stories have appeared sporadically in the past publications and his first novel, **Fortune's Mail,** was well received. His second **Truman's Glen**, is tentatively scheduled to be released by Christmas. Currently he lives in the western suburbs of Chicago, where he has lived for many years with his wife and kids and is member of the Naperville Writers Group. Working as the Grounds Manager at a suburban college, he likes to spent an off hours boring faculty members with his ideas and annoying them with what literary knowledge he has acquired.

Inspiration:1863, Redux

In our current political climate, it seems people are drifting apart. Sometimes is best to remember that it has been worse, and that the inspiration of the leaders that truly put the welfare of the country first, are the ones who will pull us back together. In hopeful that somehow remembering the words and sacrifices from our leaders of the past will begin putting us on a path to becoming a whole country again.

Inspiration: The Last Frontier

I know that one day there will be a time when the diagnoses of an incurable disease won't be a prison sentence with a framed time limit, but rather a journey to being cured. It would be pretty amazing when, in the future, a young girl's only health threat was the choice of curing her acne or smelling bad for a few days. Having raised a daughter and the 'social' choices she would make on her appearance, I thought it would add a whiff of comedy on a hopeful wish.

Inspiration: Once Upon A Time Again

The greatest day of my life was marrying my wife. Period. Without her, my personal life would have been a shadow of what it is now. Now with the last kid in high school I am excited for her and I to begin a new chapter. However, the thought of one day being able to marry her again the same way as we did the first time even if she is gone, gives me hope for the future.

Tim Yao

Tim Yao is an author of science fiction and fantasy stories. He is a founding member of the Journey, the eclectic writing group that is publishing this short story anthology. Since 2005, he has been a volunteer National Novel Writing Month Municipal Liaison for the Naperville region that serves the cities and suburbs west of Chicago. In his day job, Tim is a Domain Leader for Open Source and Software Innovations and Distinguished Member of the Technical Staff for a major telecommunications software company. You can visit his website at *naperwrimo.org/nmk.php*

His short stories and poems appear in *the Journey anthologies*: *Infinite Monkeys, The Letter, Drops of Midnight, The Day Before The End of The World, Stories from Other Worlds, Voices from the Dark, Human: An Exploration of What It Means*, and *Near Myths*.

Inspiration: Island

Ever since I heard about the *terrible floating garbage patches in the ocean*, each of which is larger than the state of Texas, and about *how fish and wildlife have increasingly been eating the floating plastics in the oceans*, to terrible consequences, I have hoped for a technological solution. Mankind created this problem; mankind must clean it up or else these problems will grow to severely impact our food supply. The *climate change-induced sea rise* is also a huge problem for the millions of people who live on islands or on the coastline.

Sadly, the solution I dream about in this poem is not (yet) real.

Inspiration: Otherness

Income inequality is a terrible problem around the world and also here in the US. Worse, many of those who have the means and the connections to help alleviate the situation are locked into news sources that effectively isolate them from the suffering of those around them. Because of this, people are seduced by the mantra that poor people are poor because they are lazy, not realizing that poor people are largely trapped by their circumstance.

Hopefully, VR games can help provide needed visibility of the problem and pierce their mistaken belief systems.

Inspiration: Free

The theme of overcoming income inequality takes a particularly urgent note with the rise of AI and robotics. We are still in the early days, but the replacement of many jobs, including white collar ones, *is looking inevitable.* One possible solution is the establishment of a *universal basic income.* Much work is needed before this solution can become socially acceptable and politically feasible.

28064153R00146

Made in the USA
Lexington, KY
11 January 2019